About the authors

Fabianca was born and raised in Tokyo, Japan.

As a young adult, her life took an unexpected turn, resulting in her spiritual awakening in the UK.

Trustfully following her intuition, and experiencing synchronicities, she now seeks to understand and interpret her various life experiences in the historic centre of Rome, Italy. From here she marvels at how the universe unfailingly guides her soul's path.

Kanon started her adult life in Japan as a high school teacher, having graduated from university in Tokyo. She also studied the process of natural healing and became a qualified Reiki Master.

A decade later after many transformations, she consciously changed her career to the banking sector. Living in Paris, America, and London, she has led a varied and inspirational life that has taken her on a personal journey with many unexpected but meaningful events. These events have led her to co-author *Light* with Fabianca, a first novel, by drawing from their shared experiences and giving them shape.

LIGHT

Fabianca and Kanon Amano

LIGHT

Vanguard Press

VANGUARD PAPERBACK

© Copyright 2018
Fabianca and Kanon Amano

A CIP catalogue record for this title is
available from the British Library.

ISBN 978 1 784654 26 9

Vanguard Press is an imprint of
Pegasus Elliot MacKenzie Publishers Ltd.
www.pegasuspublishers.com

First Published in 2018

Vanguard Press
Sheraton House Castle Park
Cambridge England

Printed & Bound in Great Britain

1

January 2016, a bright winter's day in New York. Manhattan sparkles like a crystal in the cold sunlight.

The café at 1000 Madison Avenue is quite busy with a number of varied customers.

At one of the tables is a group of three people. They radiate a certain presence, which has a strange kind of attraction. It is these three atoms of humanity, Malcolm, Suzann and Marina, that our story is about.

Malcolm appeared pale, thin and animated as he spoke:

"You know David told me he was born with the talent to sing in tune. It didn't matter where you were; prison or palace. To sing in tune is an un-buyable gift. Try and hear your own voice. It was good advice."

Suzann interrupted him:

"There is a strange vibe today like the city is in mourning."

"A great man passed on who gave a little bit of himself to everyone who could hear," replied Malcolm.

"It'll be time for you to pass on soon," observed Marina, dryly, with a knowing smile.

"You can't stay in this city too long. Now until we see you again, which I am sure we will, Suzann and I bought you this as a gift."

Marina rummaged in her bag. She pulled out a book and put it on the table.

'The Light,' proclaimed the title.

"Look," Suzann said and pointed at a young girl holding a baby, entering the café .

Malcolm didn't look. The sight of the title before his eyes caused a shift to another dimension.

His mind began to whirl and swirl and he wondered, what remains?

The last thing he remembered was the resonance of a song lyric, which kept revolving in his head:

"Where are you now? Where are you now? The moment you know, you know, you know…"

2

Malcolm, as he swirled and whirled, entered another 'now'. It took no time at all; for time has its own time to be in time with, and he was no longer in January 2016.

He entered a vortex that came out in another time. It was the autumn of 2014.

He was pacing the stage of the New York University auditorium and mesmerising his students, as he eloquently recited the lecture he had so diligently prepared:

"Everyone I am certain, once or twice in life, has seen or glimpsed, a sign that made him or her feel it was there, just for them."

His long, slightly thinning hair and sharp features, along with his outfit of blue jeans and corduroy jacket, gave him an air of eccentricity as he paced the stage, like an actor giving a soliloquy.

He rubbed his chin as he continued slowly:

"Here, off the top of my head, are some examples of what I mean. Maybe you're struggling in life in some way or the other," he raised his head at the audience. He was about forty with deep brown eyes and a well-furrowed brow.

"You have money problems. You have relationship problems and you need a way out. You are caught in a web, a tangle and cannot think how the problem can be solved."

He pointed dramatically at one of the students and continued, as if he were speaking to her alone:

"You could be passing a book store, or driving on the freeway and suddenly your eyes are caught by a billboard display. Your attention is illogically trapped, and you read something like:

"'Real success comes by converting dream and imagination into reality.'"

He directed the slogan at her and she smiled, but Malcolm's gaze had already chosen another, from his audience:

"'Twenty thousand ways to make any relationship really happen.'"

"'How beginning with nothing can help you become a billionaire.'"

"'Occult wisdom and your dream of a perfect relationship.'"

He demonstrated his cynicism of each slogan, not just with his verbal delivery, but also his physical movements. Malcolm sensed the class's amusement at his performance, so he added a few more imaginary billboards:

"'How to just think and grow rich overnight.'"

"'The law of magnet attraction and how a marriage lasts.'"

"'Coincidence and cash flow.'"

These final three brought forth peals of laughter and he smiled, sipped some water before continuing, on a more serious note:

"I am convinced from my study, of others and myself that all of us… at some point in time… have been uncertain enough one way or the other… to have been irrationally magnetised… actually irrationally believed even… some imaginary billboard slogan… is the key to solving our problem."

He looked at the interested, keen faces in front of him and their fascination, their wish to learn, warmed him.

"It is similar to what attracts us to gambling. It is born of an inherent belief in beating the odds with our uniqueness and individuality.

"To me, as I am sure it is for you, I am the centre of my own universe."

He indulged in the silence, surveying the attentive faces, before him.

"Okay that's it for the day. Any questions save them for seminars. I'm sure you've all got social networks to attend to," he added.

His lecture had gone well, his popularity was increasing, and he inwardly congratulated himself on his success.

Malcolm was Irish by birth; brought up in Dublin, he became an academic star at Trinity College, which resulted in a scholarship to the University of Michigan. He followed this by twelve years' lecturing at Berkeley in California and now, two years at NYU, where in the past six months, his career had really taken off.

It amused Malcolm as he remembered the day, six months ago, when he walked down Second Avenue and his eyes were drawn to a book entitled, 'The Light'. For someone in his position it was an irrational act doing what he did, which was to go in the shop and buy it.

However, once he read the contributors' interpretations of positivity, quantum physics and the 'law of attraction' it switched on a light. Malcolm decided to merge 'new age' concepts with traditional psychology theories in his lectures and his students loved it.

'The Light' was simply based on like attracts like and claimed there could be an increase in wealth and happiness through the power of thought, spiced with a little quantum physics. The theory appealed to his Irish humour and radicalised his approach to teaching.

It also had another effect, which was why, after his lecture Malcolm was making his way uptown.

Last week he had been invited to a talk given by one of the contributors to 'The Light'. It was sparsely attended but amongst the audience were Marina and Suzann.

He was shocked by their presence. In the past three weeks he had met them both three times separately.

He was introduced to Marina at an art exhibition. Her striking half-Japanese, half-American looks left a strong impression. He ran into her again at a book opening and then, only three days ago, at a jazz concert.

In the same time span he met Suzann, casually introduced by a French friend at the university. He met her three days later, at his new yoga class, then at an uptown cafe and now, at this talk on 'The Light'.

Malcolm tried to avoid any emotional entanglements. He had experienced too many broken hearts. He was wary of women but conscious of destiny. These meetings were too much of a coincidence. He waited until the talk was over and went to speak with them. They arranged to meet in the café at Sant Ambroeus on 1000 Madison Avenue, which is where Malcolm was making his way now.

He arrived with a sense of foreboding and a tingle of excitement. It was the first time they had intentionally met. He walked over, greeted them both and sat down.

It was then that their journey began...

3

Marina oozed class from every pore. She had a rare and unique beauty, which enabled her to either disappear into the background, or stand out like a blinding light. To begin with, Malcolm was unsure how aware she was of this trait. He was to learn she was very conscious of this magnetism and could turn it on and off, at will.

There was something ethereal and mercurial about her, as if she flowed with the current of whatever situation she found herself in.

From his previous encounters with her, Malcolm knew she was well travelled. Once she hinted at a difficult childhood, before her rise to finance director at a prestigious investment bank.

She looked trim, sporty and attractive; yet tense, as if her constant schedule, owing to the demands of her position, was always somewhere in her mind.

Suzann was more stable. She had been married since she was twenty-one. Her family had lived and owned land for five hundred years in southern France. Her upbringing and subsequent demeanour reflected this social standing.

Her childhood had been spent on a vast chateau estates. Her education was top notch; firstly at a convent then a brief spell in Geneva at a finishing school, before completing her studies at the Sorbonne in Paris, where she met her husband.

He was an American diplomat, twice her age but she was in love and he met with her family's approval. Three years ago, he received a permanent position at the United Nations and they had moved to Manhattan.

Suzann gave off a calmness and solidity in contrast to Marina, yet their opposing natures complemented each other.

"I'm so glad you came," said Marina. "I have a sense there is a reason we keep bumping into each other, like two poles of the same magnet."

"Opposites attract and repel," added Suzann.

"An atom is made of three particles. Let's say Suzann is the neutron, Marina you are the proton and I'm the electron, of the structure; a positive, negative and neutralising force as one, is that right?"

"Go on," encouraged Marina, leaning forward.

Yes, it is right," added Suzann.

Malcolm went into lecture mode. He swept back his hair and begun:

"Look at a pedestrian crossing a road and a driver who slows for him. There is an interaction. It is a law. If the driver is in a hurry, he gets anxious and blames the anonymous pedestrian. If the pedestrian feels despondent, he may cross slowly to antagonise the driver.

"The opposite may occur, the driver feels good, happy to slow down and the pedestrian smiles at him, after a fruitful assignation he or she may have had. It all takes place in seconds, but it is an unseen, invisible interaction belonging and happening in an atomic world, which forms our apparently solid reality."

"But at the same time," interjected Suzann, "on another level, we are no more than atoms of humanity, manifesting in a solar system, we have no idea about, other than as a star in the sky."

Malcolm felt strangely stimulated by Marina and Suzann. It was not physical but metaphysical. He felt they both genuinely understood a psychic influence he had never quite explored.

"At college I've started incorporating 'new age philosophy' into my psychology lectures. It's popular but I've not been touched by it. I've only looked at it theoretically… Until you two came along. My future appears uncertain, my past painful. I want to learn how to just be here and now, but have no idea how or where to start," said Malcolm.

"Me too," admitted Marina.

"Count me in," agreed Suzann.

"Hey, I've had five broken hearts and I'm full of questions," he laughed. "Who am I, what do I attract? How come some people have more than enough and others less than enough? Is humanity like a pyramid? Can I escape from being part of the base? What is the tiny thing inside me that feels unique and all knowing? Who defines a perfect, normal person? Why am I alive, in this moment, and does it mean anything? No two people physically look exactly the same, so how can two people have the same personality?

He paused, sipped his coffee and added, cheekily:

"The law of magnetic attraction and how a marriage lasts. Coincidence and cash flow."

When he mentioned the last two both Marina and Suzann giggled. The tall buildings and rushing city vibration melted before their laughter.

Marina's eyes were dark and bewitching. She wore an elegant outfit. Her face was immaculately made up. She listened intently with a look that suggested she understood and sympathised with what he had said. For a moment, to him, she shone and had a brightness that seemed to extend, like an aura, around her presence.

It was there for a moment, before it melted into a smile. She turned to look at her friend.

Suzann breathed deeply and looked at Marina, almost like she wanted advice. It seemed they had some silent communication, for Suzann turned and spoke:

"What you say intrigues me Malcolm. Marina's experience and mine complements yours. Let's order more tea and coffee."

"Good idea. And you begin your story," interjected Marina, as she summoned a waitress.

It was then that Suzann, tapping the table slightly, took a deep breath and began.

4

Suzann was of medium height with long honeyed-blonde hair and a soft, gentle skin. Her face was well crafted, and her features matched her slim, elegant figure. She wore a grey dress and cardigan. Her voice was gentle and enticing as she spoke:

"Have you ever been to Southern France?" she asked.

"No," Malcolm responded.

"It is difficult to explain its sense of history. I think it was Charles IX who first granted us land. A reward for my ancestors' part in massacring the Huguenots… Carcassonne has been a town since 3,500 B.C.; that's old. Still, its outer features are not why we are here.

"One summer's day when I was about thirteen as I was sitting with my tutor, he suddenly stood and exclaimed to the sky:

'It is possible to study the sun and moon, yet everything is within us. Inside me and inside you are the sun, the moon; the whole solar system. To understand this, one must know oneself. How do we do this? Who is this I, that calls itself me?'

"I never forgot those words, for when he spoke them something changed in me. I did have a bit of a crush on him. He was a student my mother employed, no doubt partly because of his good looks. I repeated the words over and over, until I knew them by heart.

"At school nobody tried to teach us *who* we are. I realised everyone pretended they knew themselves, everyone else and how the world should be run. When I told them the sun and moon was in us all, they thought me mad."

The wind funnelled down Madison Avenue. It chilled the brightness of the waning sun. Suzann sipped her tea and continued.

"No one chooses who they are. The family they are born into, their parents and situation. From an early age, I experienced jealousy and envy from people. Their feelings arose from hearsay and so, emotionally, I withdrew.

"My childhood surroundings were very beautiful, although my parents were not normal. They held wild parties and were morally loose. My sister, Claire, was two years older than me. I was sixteen when she went skiing with my father. They never came back."

Suzann's crystal, light-blue eyes glistened with sadness at the recollection.

"It changed my mother completely. She took to alcohol and a succession of lovers. I was sent to a finishing school in Switzerland. I didn't want to go home so from there went straight to Paris to start my degree and met my husband Paul."

After a moment of silence, Suzann sipped cold tea.

"I learnt to act according to appearance. I fell in 'love'. This word 'love' what does it mean? Whatever. With Paul I knew we could both give each other what we felt we needed "

Suzann paused again, looking thoughtfully into the distance, then turned to Marina and they spoke, momentarily in Japanese, before Suzann continued:

"My great-grandmother was Japanese. My mother always told me I was like her, so I looked into her and the culture and language. I felt drawn by it.

"Just two years ago Paul got posted to the American Embassy in Tokyo. I was able to learn the language, found forgotten relatives and studied Buddhism. I met a monk from a Temple in Takao. He was a big influence and ardently advised me, when I returned to the USA, to visit a healer who lived in Topanga Canyon.

"Once we returned I arranged to meet with her. She wasn't easy to find, for she didn't seem to use the internet, but in the end, she discovered me. One day I got a text asking if I would visit. I went and immediately she introduced Marina."

"It was very interesting," Marina remarked and melted back into the shadows.

"Her name is Kimi. She is like Marina's second mother."

"Yes. I will tell you later how we met," said Marina. "As a child Kimi was a rebel. She hated the Native American reservation where she was brought up and ran away to Detroit. She married and divorced then travelled the world. She had success and failure before returning to her roots out West.

"In those twenty years she made a journey of self-discovery and developed powers to heal, both physically and psychologically. She gained a reputation for these abilities that attracted the rich and successful, who rewarded her well. Yet one day she stopped work and became a recluse, no longer seeing clients," concluded Marina, who sat back and let Suzann continue:

"Kimi told me the spirit of my great-grandmother informed her that Marina was to be my guide. She made us a special tea, prepared as a celebration of our meeting.

"The next thing I remember was how the colours deepened. Marina transformed into a spirit. Overwhelmed, I looked at Kimi. Her eyes were like flames.

'Everything as you knew, has no place here,' said Kimi.

"I felt a panic as her words etched themselves on my psyche. I searched for a meaning and found one. I went back in time, as my tutor's voice reached me:

'It is possible to study the sun and moon, yet everything is within ourselves. Inside me and inside you are the sun, the moon and the whole solar system... to understand, one must know oneself.'

Suddenly, I heard, very clearly, everything Kimi said:

'There are parallel universes, but you must seek them. Look to your heart. Who am I? What is my desire? What am I doing and where is it leading? We appear one way but really, we are another. What is this word love?

You must travel the path of the heart. Seek freedom fuelled by inner force. The sky stretches to infinity, yet the secret lies within each one of us.

For us the world is a weird, strange, space. There is nothing other than space. Use your eyes and look to the stars. I have wandered, as you two will. We must seek both individually and together,' said Kimi.

"I remember us dancing and the sky sparkling. And I also remember Marina and I laughing as we lay on the ground, watching, for hours, the heavens in the night sky. There was a tremendous silence. I was spellbound by the beauty of this shared, extended, moment. It was intuitive. I was filled with a deep awareness of my own nothingness.

"The next day, I wondered if the previous night really existed or whether I dreamt it. Nothing was said. Kimi poured coffee. She spoke about the Law of Probability and the possibility of winning at the Casino…

It was a unique experience for both of us."

Suzann looked at Marina who nodded in agreement.

"We became bonded that's for sure. I returned to Manhattan full of questions. I was a little like you, Malcolm. Paul and I were only just back in New York, after Tokyo. That plus the experience with Kimi and Marina made me question lots of things.

About a week later I was wondering through the village and stopped at a bookstore. That book, 'The Light' grabbed my attention. I had a crazy impulse, almost a calling that I followed. I bought the book and went home, determined to find this law of attraction.

What about you Marina?"

She turned to her friend, who began to speak.

5

Marina paused and sipped her lemon and ginger tea. She was quite tall, slim and shapely, with dark, hypnotic eyes.

"I was born in Fussa, a western suburb of Tokyo. My American father was stationed at the air force base. We lived in Japan for seven years, before we went back to the States.

My father was violent. He abused my mother who hoped he might change, once we returned to the good old USA. He didn't. We suffered another three years, before we fled, inheriting only the mental and physical scars he inflicted.

"My mother tried to make up for my father's failings by working day and night, to give me a good education.

"But it was in Japan I learnt the most, before I even came to the USA. I spent much of my time, when I was in Tokyo, with my grandmother who lived beneath Takao Mountain, a place traditionally known for spirituality and mythic Shinto Gods.

"She told me stories of our ancestors and their legendary powers. In my childish eyes they were fearless and without morals, living between life and death, like avenging warriors, immaculately deceptive, cruel and without mercy.

"We went on long walks together, exploring hidden waterfalls, fields of flowers, secret places of mystical power. She taught me about herbs and healing. It was the bright morning star of my life in a way. It underwrote my spirit.

"About six months before we returned to America, she volunteered to try and heal a friend with a very aggressive form of cancer. She gave so much energy trying to heal her she had no energy left for herself and my grandmother died."

The depths of Marina's presence seemed personified in the pause that followed this introduction. What she said showed how she knew extremes, beyond most people's knowledge.

She continued:

"But I tried to forget Japan when we came to America, or put it away in my unconscious. Also, I wanted to do well at school, as my mother had invested so much in me. It was very hard for us. Kimi was so close with my mother and I went to live with her after my mother died. I was sixteen.

"Kimi knew my spiritual inheritance. She brought my grandmother and my experiences in Takao Mountain alive again in me."

Marina could mesmerise people with her emotional extremities. She did it automatically, unconsciously; it was part of her aura. She had a vulnerability and openness that was magnetic. There was something about her that, without fail, attracted people.

"Kimi helped me through university. Afterwards, I taught English for a couple of years, but, like those trained by the waterfalls of Takao Mountain, I, too, wanted to explore my inner self.

"I cast off my teaching robes, packed a bag and travelled all over Europe.

"I had been in Geneva for two years when I met my husband. He was from Chicago and we went back there only to be divorced after six months, and I didn't know what to do.

"One day I was speaking on the phone with Kimi who was telling me to stop feeling sorry for myself. Almost contemptuously, she told me to buy a copy of 'The Light'. I took it to heart, bought one and read it.

"I liked what it said about making money. At that time, I didn't have much and was realising my independence and freedom depended on it. I did what the book suggested and within two months I began a career in investment banking, which has led me here."

Marina paused. She really was a fine-looking woman. It empowered her.

"It is natural to use my charms to take advantage. I applied what I learnt from my ancestors, in the new world of finance. Outwardly, that world appears respectable, but inwardly, it was easy for me. All I did was play the same game I always had, but in a different scenario.

"I learnt quickly how to make money. The problem was I thought it would help. If I had money my problems would be solved. But money didn't help my problems. In some ways they made my problems worse.

"I want to learn. I want to see. Maybe all is destiny and already what we think is happening has already happened. Perhaps, we do not do anything. We think we 'do' but our lives are just done to us."

Her questioning lit up her aura and ambience. It was a glow like the light that attracts a moth to the flame. She was momentarily transformed and it drew, both Suzann and Malcolm.

"Revealing an iota of truth in our habitual world of lies makes people feel uncomfortable, she astutely observed.

"After all, to change means to let go of what you already know and peer into the unknown. It is easy to say but so difficult to do.

"Our tendency to just continue our habits makes change extremely difficult, certainly in my case. We rebel against that which wakes us up from sleep. As if reality was an intruder on our dream of self. As attractive as someone can be; they can be equally unattractive."

Marina stopped for a moment.

Malcolm reflected on what Marina said. He found her story remarkable and courageous for despite everything; it appeared her 'intuitive', 'seeing' self, had prevailed. She was still a real seeker of truth. He could sense it in the depth of her vibration.

"Kimi is a special person. She taught me about essences and healing; things she said that were not written in books. Often, she spoke incantations or meditated. She shared all this with me. You, Suzann, were the first person I saw, whom Kimi was as open with, as she was with me."

Marina paused and took a sip of tea:

"In 'The Light' they tell us money will change everything. I followed that and discovered that really, I was searching for something deeper, because money changed nothing inside me. It was another type of wealth I sought."

Marina stopped speaking, for opening herself up as she had done was relatively strange to her psyche. She liked to keep her inner self securely locked away. She looked at her watch.

"Goodness, we've been here almost three hours," she exclaimed. "I must leave. But wait; I have an idea. Are you both free next week?"

"Could be," Malcolm replied, intrigued at a potential proposition.

"You know me," smiled Suzann.

Marina had switched on her phone and already it had beeped six times. Her brow furrowed slightly, as she read the message and instantly called a number.

"Julia," she said, seriously, "I'm on my way."

She put her phone down and stood up, already gathering her bag.

"I must go. I have a feeling there is something the three of us must do, like it or not. Could we all get a few days off? Difficult for me as well as you… Consider it…Bye…"

In a flash she had gone.

Malcolm looked at Suzann who said, seemingly unsurprised:

"Marina is unpredictable. I wonder what she meant? Still, no doubt we will discover it. I, too, must be on my way."

She got up elegantly and kissed Malcolm farewell.

After she had gone he sat down again. Something made him feel that the meeting, which had just taken place, might alter everything. Could he get a few days off? Yes.

His heart beat faster and he wished the cold coffee in front of him was a stiff whiskey. One part of him felt like holding back and not being tempted by what fate seemed to have thrown his way.

Yet the primeval call of the spirit tempted him to pursue what destiny had thrown his way. Malcolm paid the check and went home, deep in thought.

6

The next day Suzann went into her study or 'meditation' room. As a yoga teacher she had planned for the room's emphasis to focus more on relaxation than work. There were scatter cushions, several low seats and an ambience that exuded softness and tranquillity.

She found her chair, crossed her legs and sat down placing her open palms on her knees and inhaling deeply. She did this slowly, unwinding with each breath, until her eyelids drooped closed and she began meditating.

Suzann practiced a specific format, taught to her by a pupil of an obscure French philosopher. This gentleman had practiced this path for decades. He taught her to struggle with herself. It was difficult, but she persisted, till it became a habit and now, as much as possible, it was a part of a daily routine.

Once her eyes closed she started her ritual.

She tried going around the body, getting her mind to concentrate on each limb, beginning with the right arm. It was a struggle to maintain such a level of attention. She reached her right foot, when inevitably thoughts interfered, and her attention strayed.

One moment her mind was imagining her heel. The next moment it was back with Marina and Malcolm, yesterday afternoon. The meeting clearly came alive behind her eyes, as concentration on her foot faded. She had sensed, with them, a depth and hue of perception which was a rarity. Her body tingled with an anticipation, which both elated and scared her.

She concentrated on her teacher's belief in a Law of Three, the power in a trinity with its mathematical and religious undertones of both Pythagoras and Jesus. However, as she remembered, these mental speculations did not help with sensing her right thigh. She struggled with herself. The silence deepened, echoed, resonated in a little saying she had heard that, 'three into one don't go.'

Yet two as one was nature's way of making a third.

She forced her imagination back to visualising her body, concentrating her attention on her physical presence. The words faded; she sensed her left knee. It was all to do with where the thought was. She breathed deeply and intensely.

Humans were three as one. Her teacher told her:

'We have three brains – One for the body, one for the emotions and one for the mind.'

She contemplated the possibility with her head, while her stomach felt like an ocean of emotion, as she sensed tensions in her left thigh. She entered another world where there was an abyss into which she might drop. She withdrew, wondering if Marina was fearless enough to take that step into the unknown?

Almost immediately her serenity dissipated. To contemplate a situation where she did not have control upset her.

'Beep! Beep!' insisted her phone. Her meditative images blurred at the interruption. She was glad of it. She sighed, opened her eyes and answered the call:

"Hello darling, we have to be ready in an hour. Just a reminder." It was Paul, her husband.

"Thank you honey I'll be with you soon." Suzann put the phone down.

They lived in the same apartment, which they had divided into separate suites. It had been that way for two years. The initial passion of their love affair had dwindled and died. Now they were strangers who went their separate ways. For the sake of appearance, they appeared as a happily-married couple. It was a look and partnership that suited them both. Few people were aware of it.

Suzann had only ever confided in Marina. She was secretive and kept herself to herself.

Before her interest in yoga, Suzann was a lady of leisure. Paul was wealthy and so was she, through inheritance alone. She had no need to work for anything, yet reading 'The Light' stimulated a search to get up and explore. It led her to yoga and the works of the French philosopher.

She felt yesterday might be a catalyst for even more, which excited her.

'Indeed', she thought, 'yesterday was a big step forward.'

It was time she decided to leave the study. The esoteric world needed to be replaced with something far more familiar and simpler.

She went to her en-suite bedroom and ran an essence of lavender bath. As it filled, she went to her wardrobe and carefully selected an appropriate outfit for the event they were to attend.

She laid her selection on the bed and went to bathe.

An hour later she studied herself in the mirror. She looked immaculate in her dark-blue silk dress. She smiled, selected an appropriate bag, walked out of her suite, down the corridor and into the shared lounge.

Paul, was waiting, sipping a Jack Daniels.

"You look stunning," he remarked, as he emptied the glass.

"Are you ready?" she asked, offering her arm.

"Sure am," he said, approaching.

"Beep. Beep. Beep," went Suzann's phone.

"Just a second." She held her hand out to stop him and looked at the message. It was from Marina.

'I'll read it later,' she decided.

"Okay come on," she beckoned Paul and put the mobile phone away.

Paul came forward. They were an elegant couple.

Together they walked out of the building and entered the waiting limousine, which whisked them away into the Manhattan night.

7

As Suzann meditated, Marina had just returned to her apartment on Lexington and 73rd Street. She loved the way light refracted on the city skyscrapers, as the Earth turned in its orbit toward the moon.

Marina saw herself as an atomic particle in a wave. Either dipping, rising, bursting as a huge bundle of white surf or roaring in a slipstream of epic proportions, to the shores of nowhere, receding into the all delving depths, as she descended to the ocean floor.

Here in the silence, swaying with the anemones and sea flowers, she rested until another current of hope made her rise again to the top and begin yet another journey, seeking that dry land which can never be reached.

Marina oscillated between her desire for security and her wish for the unknown. Her spirit pulled her one way while her striving for normality pulled another. She filled her life with both business and social events in attempt to minimise the temptations of that inner warrior, forged by the waterfalls of Takao Mountain. It was always there, like an inner calling.

She took off her coat, showered, and changed into a silk nightgown. She made a cup of coffee and went into the lounge, with its large window looking west over Central Park.

The silence and solitude relaxed her and tensions built up over months suddenly dropped away. She spent most of her life dealing with people and adapting to their wishes rather than her own.

To have this time, without the pressures of pleasing another, primarily, fed her deeper self...

She looked out at the spectacular hues of colour playing in the evening light, her eyes caught by the Dakota Building situated directly opposite, on the other side of the Park. It sparkled in its vampire-like vibration, drawing Marina's attention away.

Nevertheless, its existence, in that great metropolis, could not erase the seeker in her. Marina's perceptions turned inward, as the stars rose, and her attention refracted, like a prism, into the depths of her being...

Marina, like Suzann, had not chosen her life. It had been given to her. Every blow she experienced, mentally and physically, left its mark, as is the case for everyone.

She thought back to yesterday afternoon. She had felt a strong energy and bond, with both Malcolm and Suzann, enhanced by Kimi coming into the conversation.

For some reason now, and very clearly, she remembered Kimi telling her:

'The pull you have to the material world and finance works on the probability of someone getting it right. But you are here to explore more. Can you see into the invisible and make it visible? Life is a constant movement, a never-the-same sequence, a mathematical dance.'

At the time, Marina was unsatisfied, angry, trapped by the money she thought would buy freedom but which had also enslaved her.

Once, Kimi advised she must have 'patience for solitaire,' and that one day, events would move to change her situation. She felt angry, stressed and consumed by the world of materiality.

Suddenly, out of the blue, she remembered Tobias.

Kimi had asked to meet her in Los Angeles and Marina, despite difficulties, had made time.

Kimi was employed as 'spiritual advisor' to a film star on set who had panic attacks between scenes. It meant the star needed constant attention while a shoot was in progress.

The film company had provided well for them. They were staying in a house in Topanga Canyon, up from the beach at Malibu and Tobias chauffeured them to the film locations. There was much waiting around, so Tobias and Marina got to know each other.

Tobias was legendary. He had a kind, gentle face that radiated a warm, welcoming, energy. He was expansive and honest, always dressed in a long white djellaba and multi-coloured Kashmiri cap. His imported Ambassador car was unique in L.A.

Tobias was a globe-trotting Englishman. His pursuit of self-awareness had led him to explore all five continents, eventually settling by the canals, just north of Venice Beach in Los Angeles.

Marina learnt that his favourite subject was Goa, India. He was, she calculated, twenty years older than her. His stories intrigued her. He beguiled her with tales of gurus, shamans hippies and strange rituals in unexplored places. He revealed a world of white, untouched sandy beaches; quickly, she learnt his experiences had earned him a rare insight and wisdom.

The night before Marina left Topanga, she confided in him about her inner struggles. He was silent.

However, the next day, driving her to the airport, he responded.

"Marina listen and try to listen from silence. I heard what you said very clearly last night, and I've lived all over the world. The Hindus believe in reincarnation. Maybe, I've been a classic wandering Jew for centuries. But you are a high human being. Give up your belief that financial comfort is enough. It isn't, for you. Trust your inner self. Let go.

"You seek truth—it is in your aura. More than once you have doubted everything, doubted both life and yourself. It is a bleak landscape. I have been there. It is also an opportunity. Inside you are bereft of your demons, so you are open and ready for something different. One day, you will understand what I am saying."

The words Tobias said that night resonated in her being. It was as if they had been said a minute ago, not in the distant past.

Marina became calmer, aroused by the clarity of the recreated scenario.

She felt an uplifting of her spirit, just like that tiny atom of water, caught by an unexpected current of hope, coursing the ocean floor, waiting for a potential wave…

For a while, even as Marina became immersed in the world of finance, she and Tobias had remained close thanks to the digital world. However, the demands of her position left little time for self-knowledge. She developed a constant friction between her search for material power and her inherited instinct to explore the unknown. The emails and calls between them – which had been frequent – became less as her instinct became subjugated to her wish for material power. His reappearance disturbed her.

Marina knew Tobias had gone into seclusion. He left behind the Hollywood dream, for a cabin in Maine and a time of self-reflection. For three years she had heard nothing from him.

She wondered why she returned to these thoughts?

Suddenly, she felt as if she had abandoned her real self and sold it for gold. In that moment, the thought disgusted her, and she vowed that she would take the next opportunity that came her way to distance herself from the treadmill her life had become; she would grasp it.

Her phone rang:

"Hey, you were thinking of me. Synchronicity. Coincidence. The law of attraction, quantum physics, call it what you will. Are you ready?"

Marina, weak at the knees, sat down.

"Is that you Tobias?" She felt cold.

"You know it is."

"But…"

"I'd like you to come to Maine. One final opportunity to remember your spirits I won't be around to offer again."

Marina was shocked. Her face went pale at the prospect. She contemplated casting her fate to the winds.

"It is my papers that need organising. They call this place Purgatory. Where the soul goes between life and death. Ha! You'd like it, only the call of loons on the lake and no computer digits…" His voice drifted off.

An apparition of Kimi speaking flashed into Marina's mind:

"Perhaps Tobias has found a wisdom he wants to transmit to you. In the world of business your 'consciousness' is hidden behind the warrior in you. It is with you at every event you attend; be it business or pleasure. You know what another person wants… If you open up to them, they are like dogs that want to pat you. They want to own you, put a collar around your neck, attach a lead and direct your every action. Now is your chance."

Kimi faded before the voice of Tobias:

"In Purgatory there are very few people. When were you last away from the crowd? – In order to gain, on this level of life, something must be sacrificed."

There was urgency in his voice she did not understand.

"Why not ask those two friends you spent the afternoon with yesterday? Have you got the courage?"

"How did you know what I did yesterday?"

"I was in the bar at Sant Ambroeus," he said dismissively and cackled.

Nevertheless, the impossibilities swirled in Marina's mind only momentarily. For the coincidental aspect overwhelmed her normally irreversible schedule. Above all, she remembered asking if they could get three days off. Was it for this?

Had he really been in the bar? It was easier to believe than thinking he knew she had met with two friends yesterday, before it happened. The suggestion that he saw the future, plus the strangeness of the timing of his call made the demands of her work and social life pale into insignificance.

This was destiny.

Her spirit and essence took over, lifted by the possibility of an exploration of the inner unknown. She felt an irrational excitement surge through her being. What would it cost her? She didn't care.

"I'm tempted," remarked Marina.

"Everything in this life we think we do is already done," responded Tobias.

"We play out a part written in our mothers' ovaries. I already bought you a ticket for tomorrow night. You must pick it up at the airport before eight p.m. I'll send someone to meet you at Augusta when you get there. Tell your friends to wait a day or so and then join us."

Marina had an overwhelming sense that she had an obligation to her ancestry to take up the offer.

"You are very confident I will do it," she said softly.

"After I finish the call your business self will think the idea lunacy. You must struggle with it. You will come, I know. Text me when you're at the airport with the ticket. I should leave you to make your arrangements and trust to seeing you tomorrow night. Bye."

The phone line went dead.

Marina looked out the window at the sparkling lights of Manhattan.

She was as an atomic particle in a wave. In the silence of the city, swaying with the other human anemones and sea flowers, she attached herself to this current of hope, that had offered itself from nowhere.

"What am I doing, swapping my uptown heaven for a Purgatory I do not know?" she said out loud.

For a moment the room chilled. The colours deepened and in the silent, atomic, quantum dimension, she inhabited the ghost of her descendants, who replied, with a chorus of cosmic laughter.

8

"You know, your lecture on 'Personality types and Positivism,' really connected with me. The way you juxtaposed ego and invention sent shivers up my spine," said Samantha.

She sipped her glass of wine, pursed her lips erotically and uncrossed her legs, with a flirtatious swish. Malcolm was sure she wanted something.

"My husband is like a roommate. Every day I work so hard just to survive. I feel so alone. It is one of the reasons I took up psychotherapy," she continued.

"Everything is supposed to be as it is Samantha. It is one of my favourite sayings. Yet like us all I cry at what is—what do you think of the art?" He changed the subject.

"It is absorbing but not as much as the people," she responded.

Malcolm surveyed the trendy Mulberry Street Gallery. There was a rich array of guests, sparkling in their space, all made up and dressed as art pieces in themselves. They attended, as much to be seen as to regard the artist's creations.

"Could you introduce him to me?"

"You mean the artist? Sure, come on," Malcolm took her arm and walked her through the opening-night guests towards Rick.

'Hey Rick, one of my students, Samantha, anxious to make your acquaintance," he smiled, winked and left them to it.

He was well aware that his attempts at socialising were secondary to the wonderings inside his head.

Normally, he would have gone along with someone like Samantha, but tonight he was unable, for his mind kept wandering back, to yesterday afternoon and his meeting with Marina and Suzann.

Rick was a collage artist and an old friend of Malcolm's from California. He had spent a year working in Paris and this was the first showing of his creations.

They consisted of a surreal collection of photos, sketching and found objects, apparently haphazardly put together. Malcolm noticed they were popular, for there were plenty of red dots on the titles, indicating they were sold.

He was drawn into one of the works. It was three dimensional with broken bric-a-brac, glued cuttings and two women exquisitely painted, staring into the night. They reminded him of Suzann and Marina.

"Opposites attract and a territory with no borders is a dangerous place," said a voice.

It was Rick.

"After all Malcolm, we are a product of the planet. The Earth is not a product of us, even though we appear to use it as if it were just for us." He laughed.

"They're amazing, your pieces."

"It helped being in Paris."

"I'm in an odd space, Rick," confessed Malcolm. "I feel like something's going to happen to change everything. I've started doubting most things lately. Questioning what I thought to be deep and finding it quite superficial. I was talking with two women this afternoon."

"So, you're in love, man!" Rick joked.

Malcolm smiled:

"No but they have something to teach me," he admitted as much to himself, as to Rick.

It had been on Malcolm's mind and he was glad to get a moment to express it. After all, even in downtown Manhattan at an art opening, the laws of decorum still apply.

"Malcolm, so nice to see you," interrupted a university acquaintance.

"And so good to see you too," he responded politely, and his inner self disappeared as he merged once more into the social melee.

It was late when he finally got home and stumbled inside. The whole of Manhattan seemed to flash hazily outside his window. He lay on the couch and curled up. What he felt with Suzann and Marina drew him and he couldn't shake it off, not even with the copious amounts of alcohol he had consumed.

Thoughts ran, uncontrollably, through his head.

The theory he had followed all his life of Jungian archetypes was crumbling before his eyes, like the notion of associating quantum physics with riches and relationships. He was in a state of flux, his equilibrium disturbed by what should have been an inoffensive meeting in a café.

However, within he sensed an inkling of an opening door. What had begun as a billboard sign, promising the secret of the universe, had been no more than a catalyst. Yes, it had helped his career, but he sensed the possibility of going deeper. It was coupled with a fear of an unknown, anarchic cosmos, where what he knew had no relevance.

He shivered.

He saw them, in the café that afternoon, overlooking the city, not as solid objects, but in a quantum world, where all is not solid; a world where distinction of individuality, is defined only by hue, chrome and tone of colour. He visualised it very clearly; too clearly perhaps, for it shook him.

Had he been searching all his life?

Why did he have this feeling of being at a crossroads; that he should do something wild, instantaneous, instead of always needing a schedule?

"The next mad proposal I receive I shall take," he said to the darkness.

His phone replied with a beep. He looked at the illuminated message. It was from Suzann:

"Great seeing you yesterday. Can you call me in the morning, Marina and I were wondering if you can get those three days off?"

"Well, well, well," he said, switched off the phone and dropped into a dreamless sleep.

Little did Malcolm know what awaited him around the corner.

9

Marina spent the taxi drive from Augusta Airport to Tobias' cabin feeling a fool, for digitally, she had not left Manhattan. Hers was a competitive world. Finance was a seductive medium and from the moment she left her apartment, her attention was on the world of business and not her journey.

The travelling, the plane, arriving and taking another cab, this was all done on automatic pilot. Her concentration had been completely absorbed directing her associates in what to do, while she was gone.

The problem was solved when they turned west off the main highway for without warning, she lost her connection. She was wound up, tense and stressed, by a world she no longer had contact with.

She heard the rustle of the breeze, behind the smooth car's engine and sensed a vast, natural, silence. Shocked, she realised, as she woke up to her new surroundings and their immense isolation, what she had done.

She felt it like a punch in the stomach. It made her, audibly, wince and groan:

"You okay, lady?" asked the driver.

"I'm fine," she replied.

"We're nearly at your destination. It's real peaceful down here. Quiet," he observed.

She tried her phone again, still there was no connection to her other world. She felt lost. What had possessed her to take this journey? Why was she here? It was an unbelievable stupidity, she concluded. As a result of being momentarily blinded by Tobias, she was now in the middle of nowhere, going somewhere she had never been before and with no internet.

She felt it was enough. She would ask the driver to turn around and go back to Augusta. She wanted the comfort and stability of Manhattan. Her survival, her physical life, depended entirely on maintaining what she had established, business wise. Only a fool would endanger it with the illogical enterprise she had embarked on.

Without her virtual world, a well of doubt had unconsciously leaked into her psyche, leading to an internal emotional cry to go no further.

The cab was slowing. She saw a light ahead. It was too late, for already, they had turned down the drive and pulled up at the front door.

Tobias stood there, his arms open in a gesture of warmth and welcome.

"Baby I'm blessed you came. I always told you I would help you get what you really want. Now, perhaps, is time. You can't hurry Krishna. Come in, come in to my abode."

He hugged Marina and with a gesture, ushered her inside…

Marina felt a warmth issue from him. She immediately sensed his spirit was uncluttered, unimpeded by any ambitions in her material world. It was powerful enough to touch her and, without a word, lighten her burden.

"Here Tom and keep the change," he passed a note to the driver, with a flamboyant gesture, who thanked him and disappeared.

An hour later Marina's emotional state had turned a complete circle. The cabin was actually a very comfortable wooden house. They had eaten and although Marina's day had been long, and it was late, strangely, she felt wide-awake and exhilarated.

The room, Tobias took her to was lit by candles, which gave a warm, subtly sensual ambience as if there were nooks and crannies inhabited by voiceless beings.

"You know, time has its own time to be in time with. I learnt that long ago in Goa when it was a paradise and I was a hippie. Now, that is another era. Let me ask you, do you know why you are here? It is partly to do with being in time with time."

Tobias paced the floor and continued:

"As humans we are no more than little souls carrying corpses. Here is an idea for you, Marina.

"When something happens to make you feel bitter. Like you were frustrated when the internet disappeared not long ago. At any misfortune don't feel down and full of misery. Think of it differently, how to be able to bear a misfortune is actually good fortune. Everything is the wrong way around."

"I came here—"

"You had no choice Marina, but to come here," Tobias declared.

"Choice chooses the chosen. Upset what choice chooses and let it be on your head. Follow stars—" Tobias paused.

There was total silence, other than the occasional crackle of a burning log, on the fire.

Tobias seemed to be speaking in allegories that reached a place inside Marina, much deeper than those scars she acquired, in her world of social and business success.

Yet a part of Marina felt timid, alien, summoned to an event by instinct and not logic. This made her feel uncomfortable.

It was easy when seeking truth came after the indulgences of a day's business, but to face it full on, in the quiet of this Maine encounter, was another matter entirely. She felt disturbed at the inevitability and vulnerability of the situation she had put herself in; but another part of her implied that where she was, was exactly where she should be.

Tobias, though, appeared much more ethereal. He retained his generosity of spirit and largesse, which was so much a part of his character, but there was something she could not quite put her finger on, about him. It was like he was there, but also not there.

"You have come here to stop, Marina. Consider it a holiday for you to explore your natural power and second sight. You are blinded by your search for material security. It holds you back. It confounds you. It is not what you really want. Working with banks, staring at screens.

"If you're meditating in the Himalayas, no one cares about stocks and shares. There is more for you. You have no choice but to be here with me now and after this you will never be the same again. But come let me show you the lake… come on."

Tobias took a candle and beckoned her. She followed him wary of her footsteps, out of the curtained room and looking down, to avoid a stumble.

"Wow, we've come to look at the water but look at the sky," Tobias suggested.

Marina looked up.

The heavens were ablaze with flashing green, red, silver and purple streams of dancing colours. There was a wildly weird enchanted show of charged stratospheric atoms, bombarded by solar wind, creating nature's phenomenal light show; a spectrum from the heavens, a rainbow from the gods, dancing in a primrose haze that lit up the cosmos.

To Marina, the lake, her surroundings, everything, became a mass of psychedelic hue. She was spellbound, for like most of us, she had never witnessed the aurora borealis, or Northern Lights.

Tobias muttered:

"What is rare is valuable. It may be stating the obvious, but it is the truth. In space, everything is a balanced harmony, an equilibrium of equivalence. But I go too far. Don't be frightened. It's me, Tobias."

He laughed and his laughter, somehow connected to those northern lights, dazzling in the skies.

"Chaos. Let's go back inside," said Tobias.

He took Marina's hand. In a state of complete trust, she followed. Of her life in Manhattan nothing remained.

She was in the room again with Tobias and in front of her was an exquisite carpet. Had it been there before? she wondered. It disturbed her that she could not remember.

The carpet was as mesmeric as the Northern Lights, not because of its vastness in infinity, but through its intricate depiction, of the infinitesimal.

The subtle weave of geometric patterns suggested allegories and stories, of great struggles between symbolic forces, and as Marina looked closer, she could distinguish depictions of animals, both mythical and real.

Dragons, insects, hares, finches, snakes, lions, birds, and many more, esoterically hand woven; a pattern that drew Marina, somewhere she had never been.

"A soul or spirit or, quite simply the motor inside ourselves, is, like this carpet, dyed by the colour of thought," said Tobias.

"Be it the weaves of woven threads on that ancient Baluchi carpet, or that harmonic string of stars dancing in the auras we have just seen. You must trust me Marina, completely."

"Yes," she replied, though her voice, like herself, seemed so far away. Only Tobias appeared familiar, like an umbilical cord, between worlds.

"Are you ready? "Tobias asked.

She nodded.

"Good. Time for us to go on a magic carpet ride."

10

For the final time Suzann checked her tidily-packed suitcase. She added to the contents a book entitled 'Beelzebub's Tales,' before turning her attention to her vibrating iPhone.

"Thanks for calling, Malcolm. Okay. So glad you can make it. Fine. See you at JFK in an hour. I'll wait. See you then. Bye."

She ended the call, took out her earphones, and pressed the play button:

'Why,' she thought, 'am I bringing such an incomprehensible book with me?' – It had a chapter entitled, Purgatory, which, Suzann found amusing and ironic, considering where she was going.

She pressed the play button on her phone, listening to the gentle tone of the recorded voice:

"Above all, try to see that life is like two rivers that are simultaneously one. The inner river is our inner life, our essence. The outer river, the outer world we are born into and our personality that goes to meet it. They interact and entwine, mutually harmonise and disharmonise, owing to the inner river's reaction, to the outer river's flow.

"Most of us are absorbed, totally, by the outer river. Life is only about the world outside, so the inner river is ignored, not even recognised, by the consciousness of ego.

'Certainly not by Malcolm,' thought Suzann, as she pressed the pause button and once more dialled Marina.

There was no response. Suzann was anxious at being unable to contact Marina. Firstly, she wanted to confirm they were actually joining her, also because she knew Marina would be anxious without digital communication. Her business relied on it.

She wondered about Malcolm. He had a form of eccentric charm, but she was not keen on any academia. Traditional psychology was too sure and certain. As far as Suzann was concerned, the human mind was not possible to analyse, from a scientific perspective. She was indifferent to whether he was at the airport. She was excited at what was before her.

She pressed the play button on her phone and listened to the soothing voice.

"Turn your attention inside, to your inner river. Where are you going? Why are you going there? Why try to work out the future, when it is before you? Be brave, have courage and follow your instinct."

The phone vibrated, informing her that the taxi had arrived. She took out the earpiece and picked up her suitcase.

There was a touch of fall in the air. Every time Suzann drove through Manhattan she marvelled at its existence and how so much diversity of culture existed, on such a small island.

It was a thirty-minute taxi ride that she knew well and it was always filled, with the anticipation that comes from an impending flight. She arrived at the terminal, found the appropriate place to pick up the tickets and went to the café where she had arranged to meet Malcolm, wondering whether he would turn up. She looked at her watch. There were thirty minutes till the check in.

Malcolm was not far away. He studied Suzann from a distance. She looked enchanting and sophisticated. He hesitated. He knew, once he joined her, there was no turning back.

It had not been easy to get away. He cancelled a lecture and two seminars. The previous night, he had a vivid dream of Jung's diagrams from his 'book of shadow'. Some part of him was drawn by the prospect of being absurd. He was risking so much, guided only by feeling and a sense of destiny. He was uneasy, experiencing, in his opinion, 'individuation', of conscious and unconscious.

He studied Suzann's lithe form, knowing his contemporaries would laugh at self-exploration being his motivation. They would put his trip down to good old-fashioned sexual desire. A shiver went up his spine.

'After all,' he thought, 'as a man remember your Freud and spending a few days in the middle of nowhere with two attractive women has got to have influenced your decision as much as any esoteric considerations.'

He sighed, for he didn't know. He irrationally suspected something deeper at work. He decided to commit himself by quietly walking up behind Suzann, till he was close enough to smell her perfume. He bent down and said, "Boo," in her ear. There was no turning back.

Suzann, shocked, jumped and looked round, to be met by his grinning face:

"I began with 'The Light' and ended up here, in an airport. What am I doing now, I ask myself? I'm amazed we're both here." He pulled back the chair and sat down.

"Mon Dieu. You surprised me! I was wondering if you would appear," responded Suzann, offering her cheek, which he kissed lightly.

"Nervous?" asked Malcolm.

"A little," replied Suzann. "It was at the ending of our meeting, in the café. You remember, what Marina said. That's why we are both here I think. I don't know so much about your situation. It wasn't easy to get away, but I trust Marina. I know her very well. We all have a bottom line.

"Mine is that I've heard Maine can be beautiful this time of year. Also, this Tobias might interest us both."

"What interests me is the feeling I'm illogically following," responded Malcolm. "Normally I don't do that. Something logical comes along. I reject my instinct. Maybe I'm scared of gambling with my life. Most of us are," he observed.

"I've never been to Maine either so it's a first for me too. Just before I got your text, Suzann, I was thinking of doing something illogical. It was total synchronicity and so here I am," he concluded.

"Let's go check in," Suzann said, and they walked to the gate.

"You know, I'm a little worried about Marina. She obviously hasn't had an internet connection. The last I heard was when she arrived in Augusta."

Malcolm noted a slight anxiety in her tone.

"Hey, don't worry," he said reassuringly. "You can sense Marina's power from a distance. She'll be fine. The flight is in twenty minutes; we'll be there by lunchtime."

Half an hour later, they were flying through the clouds and Malcolm, like Suzann, was quietly apprehensive, as to what awaited them.

11

Marina obeyed.

Shoeless and dressed in loose-fitting clothes, she stepped onto the ancient fractal-like carpet with its signs and symbols and sat down.

Her eyes were drawn by the patterns before her.

She felt the images pulling at her being, dragging her to an inner space that since childhood had remained hidden.

Barriers, bricks, mortar and armies, which had protected her emotional universe, disappeared in the mathematical patterns of nature, unravelling before her.

She sensed all her social and business skills had no credit rating in the alien world she was about to enter.

Tobias wore a customary long white djellaba, dark glasses and on his head, a multi-coloured Kashmiri cap. Mind you, Maine was not Srinagar and so, an open fur coat loosely covered his outfit. Around his neck, he wore a long Indian shawl.

Marina, immersed in the symbolism of the carpet did not notice Tobias move from standing above her, to opposite her, until he spoke.

"You know Marina. Many years ago, I lived in England and then one day, it was just intuition, I left and went to India. Bingo and everything changed...

"I learnt we have three centres; you can see them in the patterns of three on the carpet. At school we educate and teach children that there is only a mind. Emotion is ignored. Feeling neglected, driven into solitude, locked up within itself.

"Thanks to this abnormality we are all unbalanced. India understands emotion far more than the west. There is so much to see if you look at the carpet. There," Tobias pointed, throwing back his head in laughter.

"Three Shivas and four karmas equal seven."

His head lolled forward.

Marina, while listening to Tobias, had been visited by a strange sensation that what he said was continuing a conversation begun several lifetimes ago. His face seemed to noticeably and constantly dissolve into an almost liquid form and then rematerialised with each word. His presence elongated time. She became aware that her knowledge in the material world meant nothing here. She whirled, cast adrift, spiralling out of control.

A woven group of birds in the carpet transfixed her eyes. She looked at the scene and heard Kimi, very clearly in her ear, lulling her:

'Only your deeper self is relevant where you are now. Dwell on the beauty of life. Watch the stars and see yourself. There is geometry in the song of a nightingale, music in the spacing of spheres.

'You always had chaos in you,' she continued. 'Give birth to another pattern of life. Your emotion was not killed despite all you have been through. It is time to dance like a star. To doubt is the first step to wisdom.'

Her words uplifted Marina. Tobias was speaking:

"Each animal, woven in the carpet, represents a spirit. Some soar, while others delve the depths of the underworld. All has its place. Here. Look."

Marina noticed a mountainous landscape Tobias had drawn her attention to.

"Come on. Let us go there."

For an instant Marina felt a dark infinite space that seemed to be pulling her. She had a sensation of being dragged into a spatial whirlpool followed by a sense of being sucked out the other side. She found herself somewhere she had never been before.

It was quiet. The palm trees waved. It was sandy, almost deserted, beach with an ambience of tranquillity and freedom. She wore a loose lungi over a bikini and sat next to Tobias at a bar. She watched the ocean sparkle, not far from where they were.

"Here we are, Marina. Goa, Anjuna, as it used to be in the early '70s. Hey, lucky to see it. Here my life changed. I woke up. Had my mind blown on this very spot and any thoughts of a career went out of my mind."

He looked over the scene, as he silently reflected on his lifetime.

"It's beautiful," remarked Marina.

She had let go of all she had clung onto.

Tobias got up:

"You're beautiful too. Come on." He looked down and so did Marina. There was the carpet. It magnetised her, pulled her into its dark void. She had the same sensation of being dragged into a spatial whirlpool.

She opened her eyes to find they were on a mountainside. Tobias had pointed it out, on the carpet. She saw distant snow-covered peaks. Below was a valley dotted with little villages that lined a riverside. To the left was a small, dilapidated town.

"The town is called Manali. Once I lived there. Shiva in India means 'the auspicious one'. At the highest level of Hinduism, Shiva is seen as infinite and without form. Some say the God is from here."

There was a flurry of sweet mountain wind. Marina drank it in like nectar.

"Is this no more than an illustration for you of another dimension? I am here only for a while. You keep me like a Shinto warrior between life and death, or not? We have something to do more than boast of power and parallel dimensions."

The scene faded and dissipated into darkness and that vortex sucking like a whirlpool, drawing a black hole through which she travelled back to Maine. There she was back where she began on a carpet.

"Have I been dreaming?" she questioned.

"Anything is possible," she replied to herself, laughing.

"Now you are back on familiar territory you feel more comfortable," observed Tobias.

Where we have just been is already dead. The spirit remains and resonates. You have nothing to lose any more. The worst in your life has already happened. Be clear and calm because only you alone see your own vision.

"Whatever path life has dealt, follow it from your heart. Laugh. Life is over far too soon. There is nothing impossible in a not-quite-circular world."

"I seek experience, like maybe, I would go to war. It requires me to be wide-awake and to have no fear. But this? Where have we been?"

"Hey, I remember, when you were in California," cut in Tobias, obscurely. "I watched you. Saw that if you spot potential to help then you mesmerise and magnetise them in a moment. It is in your karma and is connected to a depth of feeling. You can reveal it without a word on that level to anyone and they are spellbound. They want to get closer.

"You see desire as a weakness. Once you feel another wants you and you get what you need, you shut up shop. Put up an emotional 'closed' sign. Now it is automatic. Business is conducted that way. Your withdrawal breaks hearts. Kept in the external world, used in business, it stunts you. Die to this and be reborn."

For a microsecond Marina perceived clearly how she brought people close, with her openness. She was like a spider weaving a web. Once the subject was woven in her web, she disappeared, leaving them floundering in her slipstream.

It was so clear she understood, momentarily, why so often, relationships ended in tears for her partners, while she was left untouched and cold.

"There you see it…Wow man, she sees it! Boomshanka!" exclaimed Tobias.

He opened his arms and held his hands to the heavens.

For a second Marina saw Tobias as no longer solid.

She distinguished a form where he had occupied space, only by variations of the constantly shaping and reshaping, tiny atoms of colour. He was more apparition than human as he continued illustrating his words with movements.

"A lotus flower opens, and the day enters. We are the same. We open so all may enter. Within you, Marina, is everything; life and death, the inner and outer, sense and non-sense, male and female, being and non-being.

"You might give up the game you play. Breathe again. Be as you were born to be."

Marina felt the room turn icy cold. She dizzily sensed she was out of her body, above it, looking down. She could see her lifeless outline on the carpet. Her spirit was elated at discarding her human form. She didn't care. Her thoughts raced to the stars. She heard a chorus of voices. They distracted her. She felt weighed down, pulled. A vision of her ancestors speaking gently, coaxing her:

"Not now," they whispered. "Not now... Not now."

"You can't do that," said Tobias and his words brought her, with a bump, back to earth.

Her body was not prostrate, as she had witnessed from above. She was unmoved, still opposite Tobias, on the carpet. His eyes were fixed on hers, as he sat motionless and cross-legged.

Marina was overcome by emotion. She started crying.

"Come," said Tobias, putting his arm round her. "It is enough. Time for you to get some rest."

Marina, suddenly feeling desperately tired, took his hand and followed him to the bedroom.

12

"Noon's intensity is like an alchemical beam, turning all to gold. We are just its dust. Nothing more than tiny aspects of its spectrum," said Malcolm, poetically.

"Sounds like Rimbaud," responded Suzann. "We react to what comes at us. We do it unconsciously. Like a fly lands on your hand and you automatically swat it away. In 'The Light' they speak of the power of concentrated thought. I learnt quickly. You must have silence inside to hear your thought. It is not so easy…"

Malcolm was distracted by the sound of Suzann uncrossing her legs.

"You see," she continued. "A woman may, simultaneously, have a thought and movement guaranteed to distract a man, whatever he is doing." Suzann smiled, sweetly.

"Look," reacted Malcolm. "I'm an academic and I'm paid to know. But we assume we know because nobody knows. I subscribe to a theory of the outside world. In a hundred years' time it may be forgotten. Everything happens to us not the other way around, like now. You know for me the uncrossing of females' legs, has often, been my undoing," he concluded, humbly.

Suzann laughed.

They had turned right off the freeway and the vast empty spaces of nature stretched before their sight. It obliterated their city perceptions behind pine forests, lakes and snow-capped, distant peaks. It was one of those days when the colours dazzled the sight, grasping the mind's attention.

"Watch out!" screamed Suzann.

In front of them stood a huge stag. It looked defiantly at their hire car. Malcolm jammed on the brakes hard. The wheels locked, and they went into an uncontrollable skid. The stag, obviously satisfied with the disruption he had caused, moved majestically back into the forest.

Fortunately, the road was empty. Fifty yards down the road the car juddered to a halt.

Malcolm was shaken. Suzann took control:

"Pull over," she advised.

He took a deep breath, slowly drove to a safer spot and turned off the engine.

"Are you OK?" asked Suzann.

"It came out of nowhere like an omen. It could have been the end of us all."

"Don't worry," soothed Suzann. "Let's swap. I'll drive. We survived."

"Wow, that got me going," remarked Malcolm letting out a breath he didn't know he was holding. He recovered his composure. "It's fine. I'll drive."

He turned on the engine. They slowly pulled away and continued at a sedate pace.

"Look there," suggested Suzann, pointing into the distance. There was a sign displaying the word 'café'. Her eyes were bright and glistening.

"The internet is down," she continued, "and we need to make sure we know exactly how to get to where we are going. Let's ask. We won't get another opportunity. I reckon there are more stags than people round here," she added, laughing.

"Yea, let's check it out," agreed Malcolm.

Ten minutes later they were inside. It was as much an antique and curio shop, as a café. A smiling middle-aged New England woman greeted them.

"Hey, don't get many tourists this time of the year," she remarked.

"Well, ours is a fleeting visit and for some reason, we can't seem to get connected to the internet right now, for the online maps; so how about two coffees?" said Suzann, smiling.

"Sure," replied the owner getting up and going to prepare them.

"Where are you trying to get to?" she asked, as she brought the drinks to the table. Suzann was studying her map.

Leaving Suzann at the table, Malcolm pursued his love of browsing the store, which might contain a treasure or two. The strange encounter with the stag paled before an immediate sighting of a first edition of an Alan Watts book entitled: 'This Is It'.

He was instantaneously uplifted by the discovery. He picked it up and went back to join Suzann at the table. He decided to buy the book for his private collection. The two women, he noted, were engaged in deep conversation:

"In these parts," the owner was saying, "it can be considered something much greater; the sighting of a stag. It symbolises prophecy, the world between life and death. That's what the Native Americans say in these parts. They've lived here for thousands of years. Oh! By the way, my name is Mary. Pleased to meet you."

"I'm Suzann and this is Malcolm," she introduced them.

'Great store Mary; how much for this?" replied Malcolm. He showed her the book.

"Ten bucks."

"Sold." Malcolm sat down and gave her the money. "Everything's symbolic," he added.

The space around them seemed imbued with a silence he had not experienced in a long time.

"Here," Suzann said, pointing out their destination on the map.

"I can hear another car," cut in Mary. "Around here this time of year that's busy. I know this place you're going to and the owner— In fact, hang on."

The door to the café swung open. A flamboyant man in white walked over to Mary and hugged her.

"Hey babe, I came to pay my bill." He handed her an envelope, with a bow. "And who are your friends?"

"I can't believe this," exclaimed Mary. "This is Suzann and Malcolm and they are on their way to your house. This is Tobias."

"Surely more than a coincidence," suggested Malcolm, as he got up and shook Tobias' hand.

"Pleased to meet you and the lovely Suzann. Marina is at the cabin. I've still got chores to do. Follow me in your car.

I'll take you to the house. It's open. Give Marina a surprise while I finish up. Oh, and Malcolm, have a look through my papers, while you're there.

Tobias raised his eyebrows, for a positive response, to the suggestion.

"You look nothing like either Kimi or Marina told me," observed Suzann, still slightly shocked at the chance meeting.

He smiled. "I know I invited you. It's unfortunate but I've been called away. So, this might be hello and goodbye for now," he said. "We must go. *Tempus fugit*, as they say in Latin."

"Okay," responded Suzann, slightly taken aback. She folded away the map and stood up.

"Thank you so much Mary. We'll try and visit on the way back," she said.

"Sure, will," concurred Malcolm, "and thanks for the book."

"Hello, good-bye, and how long to the house?" He grinned at Tobias as they followed him out.

13

Marina lay alone on the bed. She slept deeply, her body splayed, motionless, other than the rhythmic rise and fall of her breasts as she breathed.

It was the only indication of life, for behind her eyes, demons that belonged in death danced their patterns.

In her dreams all was different matter.

She dwelt there in a dimension of surreal images like stellar remnants of a black star, coursing the space-time continuum. Inside, she was a child faking sleep, while her drunken American father, arriving home late, beat her with his fists and feet, dispensing bruises and terror.

Within the surreal world of Marina's psyche, fear raced through her being and an image of her mother's face, swept by winds; escaping abuse, running away to poverty, appeared as bright as daylight. It was like a portrait, in bruised black and blue, of a woman bent and broken by her efforts to give her daughter the illusion of comfort in a bleak world.

To witness Marina's lithe body, sleeping on a bed in Maine, one could not have guessed at the internal turmoil and imagery that flitted apparently haphazardly within her; an opaque distortion of real-life experiences.

Her mother worked so hard, so that Marina could learn. She did not want to waste that love. It drove her.

The image of her dream changed.

She was dancing, robotically, encircled by a billboard featuring the best academic scores, always at the top of the class, yet internally eaten, never satisfied.

The blueness of her vision dispersed and was replaced by a smiling Tobias holding a placard in front of his chest, which read:

"You live for seventy years and are dead for seventy billion."

The grin on his face grew bigger. His fingers let go of the sign he held. For a moment it floated in space before dematerialising and disappearing into an unknown atomic world.

Once more, Marina visualised in dreams.

She was cold, unemotional, prepared to do anything in her quest for success. In a microsecond, an out-of-time montage, containing her rise from poverty to become a financial wizard, passed before her.

Her virtual world was but a stage. She witnessed herself, coldly, counting enormous numbers, or playing a part at some social event, purely to further her ambitions.

But this scene of superficiality whirled before an emotional black hole. Her instinctive side sought a doorway to another dimension. A world where she felt satisfied and there was no longer that dull coldness of dissatisfaction consuming her.

Kimi appeared, like a vision, and spoke gently:

"Since a little girl Marina, you suffered, but one thing I know is suffering improves the soul. It is why you understand other people so well. It makes you question so you can understand yourself more.

"It is like polishing a gemstone or cutting a diamond for the soul. If you get through your suffering, your soul may shine like a diamond.

"Suffering makes the soul bigger and warmer. We can learn lots of things only from struggling with ourselves. You seek a safe place with your material stability, so you don't have to explore. Usually clever and successful people must struggle. Friction is required to make fire."

In Marina's dream, Kimi transformed into Tobias. She seemed to observe this alteration unemotionally. His physicality, in her psyche, held another placard that read:

"Some say the hardest thing to sacrifice in life is your own suffering."

His fingers let the sign go. It didn't drop, to the pull of gravity, but floated in space, dematerialising into an unknown atomic world. It was cold, and the Maine morning sun streaked through the curtains, illuminating Marina's body, apparently so peacefully asleep.

There was no tranquillity there though, only friction, and a sense that the portal she had always sought was there, available only for a short time-space, for her to jump into, if she had the courage. It meant letting go of seeking outside for answers and seeking them inside.

The world of ghosts awoke to the world of the living.

"Loon… Loon… Loon…" resonated loudly over the lake.

It was the haunting call of loon birds, gathering for their annual migration, which penetrated her slumber. The strange night spent with Tobias began to resurface, with each shrill pleading call, echoing over the lake.

Her body moved, and she held on to her pillow for a moment, then she sighed deeply, stretched her arms, lifted her head, rubbed her eyes and opened them; almost unaware of where she was.

Marina's head was filled by the clamour of the loons wailing over the waters. They drove her dreams back into her subconscious, as she slowly became alive and recalled yesterday.

She remembered clearly getting to the cabin, speaking with Tobias, watching the Northern Lights and the room with a strange carpet. Every recollection after that seemed disjointed and illogical.

Now in a waking state, coffee in hand, she went to the room where they had been the previous night. The carpet was no longer there. It disturbed her. In fact, as the coffee worked its caffeine, she also realised, she was alone.

Tobias was nowhere to be seen.

She was unnerved by a sense of incompleteness. She looked out over the desolate lake and watched the loons gather, swooping and crashing as they landed, while her head spun with an array of apertures, where the law of market forces and material finance held no power.

As she showered and dressed, her sense of isolation increased. She had no car. There was no internet connection, yet she was certain something had happened inside her that she could not pin down nor understand.

She felt ready for Wall Street, but was stuck in the middle of nowhere. It irked her and made her wish to be anywhere, other than where she was.

She was making another coffee, becoming increasingly frustrated, when she heard a familiar sound, which made her breathe a sigh of relief.

It was her phone, suddenly connecting to the satellite and informing her, the world of modernity was once more, within her grasp.

As she walked over to pick it up, there was a knock at the front door…

"Come in," Marina called calmly. "It's open."

14

Malcolm stood in the large kitchen/diner of Tobias' house. It was three days after he and Suzann had arrived, for they found Marina in a state of digital distraction. Something had taken place they did not understand. Either she complained Tobias was absent or dealt with a plethora of messages and emails that had built up while her connection was down. He had a permanent sense of unease since they had crossed the threshold, feeling out of depth and haunted.

The instant they arrived both recognised a change in Marina's aura. It was nothing either of them could pin down. She exuded a sense of being a flowing, ethereal spirit, yet spent her time in the digital world as if her life depended on being an audacious businesswoman.

Malcolm looked around the room. His eyes were taken by an oil painting of a distorted female. There was something both grotesque and sensuous in its composition. It symbolised, somehow, his stay in Maine. He put his hands in his pockets, shrugged and sighed, glad the journey back to Manhattan beckoned.

He looked down at the bags packed and ready for their return journey.

'And what of Tobias?' Malcolm wondered.

Tobias never returned. In reality, he only materialised through the virtual world. He cajoled, advised and directed their stay from a distance. Malcolm, under his instructions, gathered recordings and manuscripts, which covered, apparently, fifty years and five continents. What they might reveal excited him. It made the trip, in an unimaginable way, worthwhile.

A ray of sun burst into the room. It woke him to the sound of the birds. The freshness and isolation of Purgatory relaxed him. He looked outside and saw Marina and Suzann sitting on the deck overlooking the still lake. He decided not to disturb them and decided to make sure he had not missed any important papers.

Suzann also experienced a sense of unease. Her time in Maine was dominated by concern for the change she noticed in Marina. Something, she surmised, happened when Marina was alone with Tobias. It was obvious but unmentioned. Suzann felt Marina was listening to a newly-discovered flow that made a symphony within. It was tinkling, creating a new rhythm to her existence.

Yet, outwardly, nothing appeared changed.

Marina continued with her digital dialogues. She behaved like Wall Street, not Purgatory, was around the corner. Her reaction to her time with Tobias and his disappearance was to throw herself into her work. She made business her priority and couldn't wait to get back to Manhattan. She pursued the pull of the outer world as if to silence the inner voices that had been awakened during the night with Tobias. She wished they could sleep forever.

"It's beautiful here. Shame we must leave. Wonder where Malcolm is?" said Suzann.

"Tobias should have returned," remarked Marina. "I feel resentful. After all, who invites people to their house and then doesn't appear?" Marina looked out across the lake at the autumnal cascade of colours. They soothed her. She did not like it. She wanted to be busy and forget.

The reconnection to the internet gave her a means of escape. Something happened which had fundamentally altered her perceptions. It had left her unsure of everything and she didn't want to look at it.

"I'm sorry Suzann. I thought coming here I might have an epiphany. I remember seeing the Northern Lights in the sky, then you, knocking at the door. What went on in between is a blank. I should have told you earlier," admitted Marina.

"I could tell something odd happened," replied Suzann.

"If you had not met Tobias in that café he would only exist for you and Malcolm in the digital world. We can see and hear on the internet, but we cannot taste, touch or smell. We cannot perceive. I'm not sure of anything anymore," confessed Marina.

"Tobias directed us in a quiet way. Did he know before we arrived he had to go back to California? I do not know. Money can alter how I feel right now. It's been a great few days. Let's go and join Malcolm. It's getting chilly," she added, getting up.

They went inside. Malcolm heard them enter and joined them in the kitchen:

"Time to put the bags in the car and hit the road?" Malcolm suggested.

Marina's phone rang. It was Tobias. She put it on loudspeaker:

"Just ringing to say goodbye. Marina I'm so sorry, but at least we got some time together. Maybe I should have told you what happened earlier. Anyway, I went out, met Suzann and Malcolm at the store, drove back and continued to the next appointment. On the way I got a call about the plane crash. They say its touch and go whether anyone will survive. My brother was on it. I'm at the hospital now. The moment they told me I forgot everything and headed straight for the airport. Shit the phone's crackling, bad line I better go. Have a safe trip back."

It went dead. Suzann looked at her watch.

"So finally, he explained," said Marina, relieved.

"His brother. I hope he'll be OK," remarked Suzann.

"Time to go," decided Malcolm. He packed the bags into the car and they drove off.

Thirty minutes later they reached the highway to Augusta. It seemed comforting somehow to have left the desolation of Purgatory behind them.

"You know one thing that was really weird on that road…" began Suzann.

"I know what it is," cut in Malcolm.

"What?" she asked.

"That café where we met Tobias. I didn't see it."

"Nor did I," added Suzann.

"Well, I wasn't there, so I couldn't know, but we didn't pass a café," cut in Marina. "Anyway, thank you both for coming on the journey. Look," she pointed.

In the distance the glow of Augusta stood out amongst the lakes, forests and mountains. All of them felt drawn by the sight of urbanisation.

"This whole event will take time to digest," commented Suzann.

"Sure, will," agreed Marina.

Several hours later, Maine was behind them. They were in a cab nearing the Lincoln tunnel, after their flight from Augusta. In the distance, Manhattan, towering to the sky, glowed with its unique beauty.

Once under the Hudson River it was as if, for them all, Maine and what had taken place there, also went underground. It became submerged in their subconscious. Indeed, by the time they reached the Village and were dropping Malcolm home the familiar world of Manhattan had enveloped them.

'Beep, Beep,' went Marina's phone, as Malcolm got out of the cab. She looked at the message, dropped the phone and cried out.

"What is it?" said Suzann, alarmed.

Marina picked up the phone. The message read:

"Couldn't tell you till I was absolutely sure. It was Kimi, not my brother, who was on the plane that crashed."

15

Two days after returning from Maine, Suzann went shopping at Bloomingdales. Retail therapy always helped in times of vulnerability and stress. She had gone to town, buying for the sake of it and glad she was able to. It gave her a sense of protected abandonment.

Afterwards she went home. She left her baggage in the hallway and went into her meditation room.

Here she rearranged some cushions, sat down with her legs crossed and opened her palms, resting them on her knees. She took a deep breath, closed her eyes and began her inner exploration.

"How do you value anything?" Tobias' voice spoke very clearly in her mind.

It shocked her, but she did not flinch, nor move. She only reacted internally. "By money," she silently responded with a smirk. "Society deems it so, as a means of exchange, a symbol to represent a human's level of survival.

"That's why the book 'The Light' is so popular. People striving for security and seeking the mystic, to line their pockets with coinage," responded Tobias.

Suzann opened her eyes. She was scared at how real these imaginings of someone she hardly knew had become. It unsettled her enough to check the room, but it just confirmed she was alone. Once again, she closed her eyes. This time Kimi appeared and spoke very clearly:

"Is life and death to do with making money? Are we on the planet to compete for ownership of what created us? What does a human being own? How many millionaires and billionaires are as unhappy as the financially poorest? When you are poor you only have here and now. The future and past mean nothing. The rich live in a world where each day is planned before it arrives. They live in the world of 'never now'. They are imprisoned by the appointment book."

Suzann felt a welling of emotion as she visualised the ghost of Kimi. She felt her loss so much. There were tears in her eyes, but she suppressed them.

Something had happened to her in Maine and it disturbed her.

It was related to the value she put on materiality. There seemed a paradox, for she was questioning what wealth really was. After all, her meditations continued, she sought for something else.

Prophets, priests, monks and seers sought non-attachment, even to themselves, as a form of achievement. The world of art was full of creators, whom, while alive, were vilified and yet after death, in another generation, were praised, revered and remembered, long after those who acquired gold through material need and ambition.

Suzann felt cold, unbalanced by a fear of the unknown. Something triggered in Maine. She breathed deeply, imagined the silence by the lake. It calmed and comforted her. The death of Kimi filled her with a gentleness and peace.

Her mind became filled by an image of rain falling gently and amongst the many droplets were some that were brightly coloured. They shone as they fluttered and fell towards the Earth.

"Here. Look. Those coloured drops can be caught. It makes no difference whether you catch them. They contain the spirit of Kimi. Can you pay?" said a voice in her head.

Suzann wanted to mourn her friend. Kimi's death had only just begun to sink in. It had been a huge shock and to sit still was a struggle. It felt like an eternity she had been meditating. She held out her hand to catch invisible raindrops. A thought came that made her open her eyes with a start:

'The price of life is measured out in dreams.'

She looked at her watch. What seemed like eternity had only been six minutes. She felt a disharmony, a mental imbalance that she shook off when her phone rang. It was Marina. She picked it up:

"How are you?" She asked calmly, knowing that Marina would not be calm.

"I'm so sad Suzann. Many people want my attention. It's crazy. I've hardly slept. I think I caught a cold. Yesterday I took some pills and slept all day. I couldn't concentrate when we met. I know I tried to be fine. I wanted to say how really sorry I am." Her voice trembled with emotion.

"Concentrate on now, Marina. Tomorrow morning I'll pick you up in a cab and we can go to JFK together. Once we're in California we can celebrate Kimi's life and help lay her to rest." Suzann choked back her tears. She felt she must keep her emotions in check and be brave to support her friend.

"I must go, Suzann. I'll see you tomorrow. So much to do. Bye." There was a tension in Marina's voice that betrayed her inner turmoil.

Suzann felt an urge to go out and followed it. She had forgotten to buy her favourite perfume. Five minutes later she was walking down 5th Avenue. A voice called that stopped her in her tracks.

"Hey, Hey, Suzann." It grabbed her attention above the noise and impressions of central Manhattan. She turned around and stopped, her mouth open.

Towards her walked a man and by his customary attire she instantly recognised him as Tobias.

"Wow, I cannot believe this. My last thirty minutes in the city before I fly off and I meet you… There is no such thing as coincidence!"

Tobias threw back his head and laughed as he greeted her. Suzann felt as if his mirth lifted a weight from her.

"Come," he continued and took her hand.

In another five minutes they were sitting in a quiet café.

"You know Suzann," he said. "Everybody is different and in being different we are the same. People forget that. After all no one can occupy the same space at the same time. The nearest they get to it is when they fuck."

He sipped his coffee and continued:

"Did Marina ever tell you what happened when we were together in Maine? I can tell by the look on your face she didn't. It is not important. How has she taken Kimi's death?"

"She works harder. She gets lost in feeling she is needed. More than ever she is justifying life by making money." Suzann was shocked at what she said.

"Ha! Just as I thought, she should let go and trust. Life will support her. She has awareness and needs to understand it. Don't tell her we met!" He opened his palms in a theatrical fashion and looked at his watch.

"Are you not upset by Kimi's death?" Suzann enquired.

"No. I do not believe in death as others do. I catch coloured raindrops." Tobias held her eyes as he spoke. She felt as if time slowed. The microsecond it took for the words to be uttered was followed by a pause. It elongated into hours despite, in real time, being no time at all.

Tobias brought her back:

"I think you understand what I'm saying, well a little," he added and smiled.

Suzann felt herself return to normal.

"Now, I must go. Amazing to bump into each other as we just have done, especially, as I only came to Manhattan for forty-eight hours. Anyway, I will see you tomorrow in California, won't I?"

"Guess so."

Soon they were back on the sidewalk, amongst the hurly burly of Manhattan. Tobias hugged her and once more held her with his eyes.

"This is a beginning for you not an end."

And with those words he disappeared into the crowd.

16

The evening after returning from Maine, Malcolm stepped into an art gallery opening to which he'd been invited. He was almost overwhelmed by the activity of the occasion.

However, the buzz of general conversation, the music and ambience of the attending glitterati did exactly what he hoped. It distracted him from contemplating, even further, his experiences with Suzann and Marina, in Purgatory.

He found his way to the bar, took a glass of champagne and went to join a group of acquaintances.

"Hey," he said.

"Malcolm, where were you? You missed Phoebe's exhibition, 'Junk, Joy and Jung'. It was amazing," enthused Mark, a fellow psychology lecturer.

He gestured towards a well-dressed, thin woman, with a pale face and bright red lips.

"Pleased to meet you," Phoebe said.

"Malcolm," he responded, shaking her hand and adding:

"In all chaos there is a quantum. In all disorder a secret order."

"Wow. Now that is an amazing statement. My work's chaotic and full of disorder," she responded, with a twinkle in her eye.

"Yea, you should have seen the red dots at her show. Phoebe can storm the modern art world," concluded Mark.

"With Junk, Joy and Jung!" laughed Malcolm.

He raised his glass and drank to her impending success while vaguely perusing the paintings.

A canvas illustrating a never-ending, imploding circle, caught his gaze. He was transfixed by the 'gyre' that sucked him in. As he stared at the creation it transmuted and, once more, the sight of the lake in Maine, its strange ambience and unknown vibration, returned.

'Even here I can't escape it,' he thought.

"So, you're an expert on Jung," asked Phoebe, diverting his attention back to her.

"Yea I am. He has something for every occasion. Hey, it is even why I missed your show."

"Really? So why was that?"

"'Anyone,'" quoted Malcolm, "'who wants to know the human psyche will learn next to nothing from experimental psychology. They would be better advised to abandon exact science, put away their scholar's gown, bid farewell to study and wander with a human heart throughout the world.'"

His voice trailed off towards the end. He realised how appropriate it was for where he found himself, right now.

Phoebe took his arm.

"Come on, I'll introduce you to the artist," she said and led him away.

Two hours later they stood together on Mercer Street. There was a brisk wind. Phoebe held her coat tight but moved closer to him.

"You know you're a crazy guy. I mean half the time in there I got the idea you were somewhere else. Not with me and for me that's unusual with a man I like." She moved closer.

He sensed her warmth and openness. He looked in her eyes. She swooped and kissed him full on the lips.

"Are you sure you don't want another drink?" she asked, cuddling him.

"It's real kind but I've got to say no. I've got so much work to catch up on and three lectures tomorrow, but how about later in the week? Hang on, I'll get my phone."

Malcolm disentangled himself from her grip and pulled out his phone, took her number and dialled it.

"So now we've exchanged numbers, it's home for me. We could meet at your studio and you could show me your work?" He suggested

"Okay Jerk," she joked and disappeared back inside the gallery.

Malcolm walked home and half an hour later was fast asleep in his bed.

His rest was invaded by a series of surreal dreams. He felt he had crossed a threshold. A vision of his mother speaking to him as a child of eight or nine, invaded his imagination.

"Be careful Malcolm… You can know too much."

The words resonated and for the first time he understood their implication. But the moment he knew he ceased to know, for his mother merged, transmuted and became Marina.

She was dancing, and her dance transfixed the audience with its lithe, sensual movement. He, also, was entranced. Once she noticed him she moved in his direction. He felt himself imploding, being pulled somewhere the spirit had yet to encounter. Her lips, close to his ear, as she gyrated in front of him, spoke:

"A healthy person does not torture others. Usually it is the tortured who turn into torturers."

All Marina had told him of her childhood and her desperations took on another meaning. Her passions and extremes, the prison of her own making, became, momentarily, revealed.

Suddenly, he was no longer in her space, but on an unknown beach, in an unknown bay. It was calm, and the little waves lapped the shore, while he stared at a huge rock. It looked like a giant king on his throne.

"So how do you deal with that dance?" asked a voice.

He turned and found he was next to Tobias, whose eyes were bright red, burning like they were on fire.

"With serenity," added Suzann calmly. She was dressed in a skimpy robe that barely covered her slight bikini.

"In order to learn and understand what you must go through don't fight it. All is only as it is supposed to be," concluded Tobias.

In an instant, the scenario transformed. He was now silently sitting with Carl Jung, somewhere in Switzerland. For a moment, they viewed the Alps. The silence of the great psychologist, with his fuming pipe, imbued him with a certain peace.

Next, he was whirling and swirling back to the kitchen in Maine, sitting with Tobias, who said:

"We cannot avoid destiny. We all may try and believe we have a choice, but choice chooses the chosen. Better to follow stars. It is your destiny and Marina's and Suzann's, and mine. There is no escape from the inevitable," he added thoughtfully.

"But I want to turn back!" Malcolm screamed.

There was no one to hear. He was alone and unmoving in Manhattan, to all intents and purposes, fast asleep.

Inside he was back in Marina's presence as she whispered, again, in his ear:

"Your visions become clear when you look into your heart. If you look outside you see only dreams. Look inside and wake up. I irritate you. You want to run away. Your instinct tells you my irritation can lead to an understanding. Your personality and dreams tell you to react to my irritation by ignoring me. Ignorance, as we know, is bliss."

How clear was her voice, how well defined and then, like a space invader, he heard an alien call.

A signal from another universe beckoned, from a land he barely recalled. It was his mobile phone alerting him, like a fond servant, to his daily duties. He struggled with it, but the stark images blurred. He became pulled, tugged from his centre, to the world of apparent wakefulness.

His eyes opened and took in the new day, although his mind still clung to the surreal series of dreams he had just experienced. There was a strange taste in his mouth and he felt slightly groggy. In fact, he decided, he didn't feel well at all.

Nevertheless, as he usually did, he got out of bed and stood up. He had an overwhelming wish to return to the images he had while sleeping.

For some reason he had no wish to see the day.

His legs wobbled. He was light headed.

A dizziness followed by blackness enveloped him and like a rag doll, he crumpled and collapsed, unconscious, on the floor.

17

"Death is like a celebration, then?" remarked one of the mourners to Suzann, at Kimi's wake. He was vaguely familiar, but she was unsure where they had met before.

"Yes,' she responded. She could sense his interest and continued.

"Some Japanese Zen masters know in life, when they will die. There is a story, would you like to hear it?"

"Yes," he replied intrigued.

"Well, one day a Zen Master called together his followers and told them

"'I have noticed, during this last week, my energy fails. No need to worry. It is the approach of death.'

His followers, disturbed and anxious, replied: 'What does it mean for us; how must we go on living when you are about to die?'

'They are both the way of all things," the Master replied.

'But how can one understand two such different states at the same time?'

'When it rains it pours,' the Master smiled, then calmly died.'"

Suzann completed the legend and sipped her drink. She could feel the presence of Kimi whose spirit imbued the room.

She carried on speaking, as much to herself as to the stranger, by her side.

"Death is just a beginning, a transition to another existence within an eternal circle. Breath is infinite but not the body that breathes. This holds the possibility of forever. Already, Kimi's karma is actively seeking her next incarnation.

"All physical formations are impermanent, subject to rise, to fall and to decay. We are liquid, each making for the ocean. A funeral liberates the soul," she concluded.

High white clouds raced across the skies. They sent shafts of shadow and light dancing over the vast, dried up Topanga creek, beneath them. The house, built into the side of the Malibu Mountain hummed that day, with the celebration of Kimi's passing.

"Now that is fascinating what you say. Revealing even. My name's Frank Whitely and you?" asked the stranger.

"Yes, sorry. Suzann," she responded and smiled, although she was slightly concerned. Since the ceremony, she had not seen Marina.

There had been no sight of her.

Marina, in the moment Suzann thought of her, was fuming and about to explode with anger.

She was seated, with Tobias, in the front of a broken-down Karma Cab. Steam was pouring from the open bonnet of the Ambassador car, like a smoking volcano.

Marina desperately attempted to control her feelings. The past fortnight had overwhelmed her. The intensity and battles at work meant spending often eighteen hours a day, in her office. Also, on a deeper level, she blamed the visit to Maine, for compounding her problems. It symbolised why she now sat, helplessly, on the Pacific Coast Highway, having just buried her second mother.

"So, what's the problem?" joked Tobias, insensitively.

His bland tone was the touch paper that ignited her frustrations:

"The problem? It's simple, the problem is you. We arrived, you took us to the hotel and disappeared. Miraculously, you came and took us to the ceremony. Next, you persuade me to let you drive me to the wake. We break down and… not to mention what happened in Maine? Perhaps I do not pay enough for your Karma Cabbie." She spat the words contemptuously at him.

"Hey look, don't get emotional with me" responded Tobias, agitated.

"I bloody well will," Marina argued back. Her eyes blazed.

Marina opened the car door, took her bag and started walking down the road. To the left of the highway the mighty Pacific crashed. Suddenly Tobias was in front of her:

"Stop," he commanded and held her wrists tightly. "Come to the car."

He led her firmly back, slamming the bonnet closed, before they both got in. Marina broke down hysterically. She felt completely alone, bereft of her demons. Tobias put his arm round her gently.

"It's okay," he whispered, "You can trust me."

"It's everything. Kimi dying, my work, that trip to Maine everything in question, a state of flux." She sobbed hysterically and uncontrollably. He held her, comforted her, till he sensed she had calmed a little.

"Let's try again, huh?" Tobias said gently.

He let go of her, turned the ignition and the engine sparked back into life.

"See there's nothing wrong with a breakdown if it gets you started again. I can't stay at the wake. I've got a job to do. It's so difficult to be unemotional."

He leaned over and held her. She forgave him.

He sensed it, pulled out onto the road and drove off up Topanga Canyon. Fifteen minutes later they stopped by the house.

"Look, in two hours can you meet me at the West Beach Bar in Venice? We need to talk more about Maine; about what happened when we were alone. That is if you want to?"

"I certainly do," replied Marina. She got out the car and went to find Suzann.

18

At the wake, Suzann was listening to her new friend:

"Did you know legend has it," said Frank, "that Topanga used to be a Native American burial ground? It's sacred like Kimi, a remarkable woman. Everyone who was anyone in this town and beyond wanted her attention. She had a way of relaxing a person, calming them, just by her presence. It's a great rarity to have that power. But Zen seems cool to me. They're not fighting over anything like some of those other religions. What do you do? For work that is?"

"I'm a yoga teacher in Manhattan," replied Suzann. "Kimi was my mentor. Certainly, her influence changed me. She awoke something psychic. But I'm sorry. I'm sure we've met before?"

Frank laughed:

"I get asked that question most days. I've got lots of different answers too! But I'll be honest, you've seen me on the TV."

"Got it," interrupted Suzann, her eyes lighting up. "Gene Cooper from San Diego Detectives!"

"Sure am," he smiled back, proudly.

"Wow," he added looking over her shoulder. Suzann followed his eyes. Marina, looking very sophisticated, was walking towards them.

"Hey, wondered where you got to? This is Frank," said Suzann, relieved to see her friend.

"Nice to meet you, Frank I'm Marina. Can I borrow Suzann for a minute? I promise I'll bring her back," she smiled.

"Don't go anywhere; I'll be back," said Suzann.

Together they found a space and sat down.

"Sorry Tobias' car broke down. We argued, but I feel better for it. I'm inheriting something, it began before we went to Maine. It has nothing to do with what I've acquired from my outer existence. In here is where it is."

Marina pointed to her middle to illustrate the definition. For a moment there was a stillness and quiet, despite the many people.

"I can feel here, Kimi's gift, her inheritance. Look around there are many wealthy, famous people here. What is really valuable; money? Is that what we all respect the most?"

Suzann understood. It touched her, and she knew that just by listening she gave her friend some warmth.

"And now, I must put on a face and be sociable." said Marina, straightening her back. "Tobias asked me to meet him at a place on Venice Beach in two hours. Shall I go?"

"Whatever you decide; I think I can get Frank to be our chauffeur," winked Suzann and Marina grinned.

Two hours later Frank's limo was driving them along Pacific Avenue. It turned right onto North Venice Boulevard and stopped. A parked Karma Cab indicated Tobias was already inside.

"There's a place I know in Santa Monica, Suzann. You and I could get a meal there, and afterwards we can come and pick Marina up if she likes? Give her some space with this Tobias. Good idea?"

"Great idea Frank and very diplomatic," remarked Marina.

"Be careful," smiled Suzann.

"Of course I will be. Don't worry," replied Marina confidently.

She stepped outside.

Ahead of her, the ocean glistened, bathed in a green-blue hue, refracted by the waxing moonlight. The rhythm of pounding waves soothed her and with a sigh of slight anticipation, she entered the bar.

19

Marina was thankful Frank offered her an alternative to being reliant on Tobias for a ride. She liked to keep her options open. Her heart was still heavy, despite the politeness she summoned at the wake.

Tobias sat at the bar counter and his face beamed when Marina walked in. He had changed out of his usual attire and now wore a plain white, freshly pressed suit, with a floral, collarless shirt, offset by a pair of large dark sunglasses.

The place had a soft, gentle, ambience. Marina, smiling, walked gracefully over to join Tobias. She sat on the tall chair and with a swish of silk, crossed her legs.

She had, during the past few hours, decided to withdraw from any further explorations of her psyche. Since the cremation she had a sense of being out of depth, going into a dark, unknown space. It intrigued and terrified her simultaneously.

Indeed, as she sat down, she was confident of opting for security and she was convinced that her status, her work, the world of finance, although totally consuming, was safer than any world Tobias had to offer. All Marina required, before returning to Manhattan, was to satisfy her curiosity as to what happened the night before the arrival of Suzann and Malcolm, in Maine.

Tobias was drinking a multi coloured cocktail that caught her eye:

"Don't worry," he anticipated, "I'm staying only a walk away in terms of distance. I'm not driving anywhere. I can drink what I like! Come on, join me." He gestured to the bartender and continued:

"Venice is my favourite part of Los Angeles; Kimi's too. Sometimes she'd set up a stall at the bottom of Windward Avenue and read tarot cards or meet clients in the Sidewalk Café. This whole area is a replica of Venice in Italy. Made by someone with so much money they didn't know what to do with it.

"The canals and wooden houses are within the sound of the ocean, it's weird. I'm staying in one around the corner. Carroll Canal, like to take a look? Everything starts with an aim at freedom and ends up being a prison. Or is it the other way around?

"Thanks, Charles," Tobias concluded his monologue, as the bartender set down their psychedelic looking drinks with a flourish.

"Each mortal thing," began Tobias, quietly. Marina had to listen hard to hear him.

"Does one thing and the same, deals out that being indoors where each one dwells. God I'm drunk."

Tobias took off his glasses.

Marina looked into his eyes. His words stirred up her insides. Their resonance excited her. She sipped her cocktail, absorbed and mesmerised by Tobias's voice:

"You don't want to come to my house that is… I'm guessing… I think you've decided to dismiss any insights gained during the last few weeks. You wish to return to a world you feel comfortable with. As if one may turn back time. If only it was that easy."

The drink warmed her:

"Yep back to Manhattan to bottle up my genies," she replied, with a sigh. "Time to put away mystics as of today."

"I agree," interrupted Tobias. "You must withdraw. It's too dark for you, this unknown."

"No… It isn't," she refuted, automatically.

Suddenly Marina realised how careful she had to be.

The part of her, so uppermost in her consciousness, when she had walked into the bar, had faded completely in the presence of Tobias. Her perception had altered with each sip of her drink. Her original resolve was no match for those unseen energies, invisibly dancing over Venice Beach.

The phosphorescence Marina saw reflecting on the ocean, before joining Tobias, was a luminescence which does not immediately re-emit the radiation it absorbs. So it was for Marina. Her motion of time had slowed, elongating her moment, making her open and vulnerable to a dark energy, a strange attraction to transitions, in an atomic quantum leap, of cosmic proportions.

"The world of 'Is' is wherever you are. Can either one of us prevent our doom? Our personality may argue with destiny, but logic is never enough," declared Tobias. He made a gesture like he was surrendering to the inevitable.

"I see you liked the cocktail," he observed, contemplating her almost empty glass. It's called a 'Cool Breeze'. Vodka, triple sec, mixed with crushed ice and topped up with champagne. Guaranteed to trip you to Mars! Two more," he ordered, soberly.

"Beep… Beep… Beep," went Marina's phone. She read the message. It was from Suzann: 'What would you like to do? Shall we pick you up?'

"Here's another Cool Breeze drink it with Kimi in mind," advised Tobias.

She looked at him. Took her glass and raised it in a toast:

"To the Spirits," Marina said, and they drank deeply.

Meanwhile Suzann, charmed and dined by her admirer Frank, sat with him, watching the waves pound the shore in the near full moon.

It was a sight Suzann revelled in. The vast enormity of water, crashing in huge white waves, lit by a lunar light and a sense of sharing, with a near stranger, tempted and exhilarated her.

Frank spoke:

"I first came here as a kid. My dad told me the same ocean stretched along the whole coastline. To me it stretched for an eternity. Since then, sometimes I come down here just to stretch. To shut out distractions, I go into the depths. Try and re-snatch life long dead from a roar across infinity.

"Hey. Now I don't sound like a detective at all. So, what to do? Huh? Shall we go and get your friend, Marina? Or visit my home in the Hollywood Hills?"

"I'll text her. See what she says. It's so beautiful here. I guess the moon helps," said Suzann as she wrote her message.

"When do you go back?" asked Frank.

"Tomorrow afternoon, why?"

"And you're not going to visit Beverly Hills?" He sounded incredulous.

"I came for a funeral," she responded.

"Yes. But come *on*. Will you get the chance again? I like your company," he added, as she pressed the send button.

"Let's see what she says. But hey I'm married."

"And I've got a mansion," responded Frank.

"Mulholland Drive tempts me," admitted Suzann.

Her phone rang. It was Marina.

"How's the evening?"

"It's great," replied Suzann. "Do you want us to pick you up?"

"It's ok I'm going to stay. Tobias has a house around the corner; let's trust to destiny."

"Both of us. Have a good night," responded Suzann and put the phone down.

She looked at Frank:

"So, you are right. It's the Hollywood Hills and Rodeo Drive in the morning."

He laughed, paid the check and they walked off, towards the waiting limousine.

As Suzann and Frank entered their limo, heading for the Hollywood Hills, at the West Beach Bar the conversation continued:

"I knew you'd relent. You're too inquisitive. Shall we go?" said Tobias.

"Sure, why not?" Marina answered.

Five minutes later, they were outside, staring at the stars.

"Come on. We have work to do," said Tobias.

"Work?" she repeated, incredulously.

"Yes, not your kind of work, *my* type of work. It's time to remind you of Maine."

Marina smiled inwardly. The drink had dampened any fears and she felt relieved that Tobias might reveal the mystery that had plagued her since she went to Maine. She quickly caught up with him.

"I'm looking forward to it," she said, confidently.

On the other side of the USA, in New York's Sinai Hospital, Dr Cleaver and Dr Grad were briefly discussing Malcolm, who was being rushed to an operating room, for emergency surgery.

"One of his students found him. He had collapsed. I think he needs a new valve perhaps? As in yesterday, what do you think?"

"He'll be lucky to live but let's get washed up anyway."

Malcolm, lying unconscious on the stretcher had no idea of the drama being played out, nor the danger he was in. He was caught, in no man's land, balanced precariously on a tightrope between life and death.

20

For Marina, the walk to Tobias's little cottage on Carroll Canal was like a scene from an absurd theatre production. In the moonlight they walked a few blocks. They then crossed a small white bridge. They entered the property, via a little gate and through a garden of tropical plants, with a palm tree as the centrepiece of the well-manicured lawn.

The wooden house was situated on the edge of the canal, yet within the scent of the salty sea and the sound of beating surf, rhythmically and eternally searching for the shore. There was something so illusory in the whole creation. To Marina it represented all Hollywood stood for, in terms of materialising a world of dreams as solid, immutable fact.

"Come in," Tobias beckoned.

He stood on the threshold, holding the door open.

Marina entered. She was surprised for, from the outside, the house appeared tiny and yet once inside, it gave the impression of infinite proportion.

"Optical illusion,' remarked Tobias, knowing her thoughts.

"It's made that way. Here let me show you. Come into the kitchen."

The room looked like a capsule or tube. From the outside of the house, such dimensions appeared impossible. The premises had not the space to contain such size. It defied the laws of physics, yet Marina accepted the irregularity of proportion without question.

"I'm not here for architecture or the magical alignment of artistic temperament," snapped Marina. "I'm here to carry on where we left off. We began some weeks ago in Maine. Remember? I have a vague memory of what transpired. But how can I speak of what I'm uncertain of myself? In casual conversation you have avoided me… Mix another drink," she ordered.

"Let's go into the lounge. I'll explain when we get there," replied Tobias.

"Come."

Marina followed Tobias into a room.

He lit some candles to illuminate the space and their light revealed an apparent vastness, which once more defied all sense of proportion. Yet as soon as Marina entered the room she lost all interest in dimensions.

Her attention instantly fell on the exquisite carpet in front of her. She recalled it from Purgatory, Maine and within its phantasmagoria she remembered all that had taken place. The subtle weave of geometric patterns dissolved time. The dragons, insects, hares, finches, snakes, lions, birds, and many more, esoterically hand-woven images, whirled her back to where she was the last time she encountered them.

She did not notice Tobias quietly smiled as he watched her.

Entranced, Marina removed her shoes and sat down on the fractal carpet. A woven pattern drew her into its landscape. She heard the voice of Kimi whispering very clearly in her ear:

"Only your deeper self is relevant where we are now. Dwell on the beauty of life. Watch the stars and see yourself. There is geometry in the song of a nightingale, music in the spacing of spheres. We all have chaos within us. It is time to dance like a star. To doubt is the first step towards wisdom."

Kimi's presence was so alive that for a moment, she forgot about Tobias. Slowly he came back into her sound and vision.

He sat opposite her on the carpet. He still wore his white suit but looked older, much older and spoke like an ancient Buddhist Priest.

She listened intently as his words resonated deep inside her.

"I can understand how certain people who in a rarefied atmosphere, spend their whole time sitting cross-legged like we do on this carpet, staring into what most other people might perceive as just being empty space."

Tobias paused and for Marina, in that moment, her spectrum seemed to deepen. Her whole hue intensified. Now, she remembered their last journey together. Time slowed down and what she usually took in, during a second, intensified. She heard Tobias continue. His voice sounded elongated:

"Be forewarned. No space is empty. That which does not appear visible to one's own eyes may well be visible to another being's. I wonder what the Sandpiper sees while foddering by the ocean's edge? How does his eye see the dance play of crystal sunlight shining on his catches? His life force... playing with water and fire..."

His words were illustrated by a vision on the carpet. She saw an image of the tiny bird, playing with water and fire; dancing, each element negating and verifying the other's existence, eternally.

The vision faded as Tobias continued.

"Those men who sit cross-legged for years must catch e/motion in their visible. They let all things pass and attain strangely respectful states in rejecting the physical for the metaphysical, each to his own realm. Knowing there is more to life than meets the eye... Bodhisattva."

Tobias altered as he finished. To Marina he became wreathed in a visible aura that dispensed beams, particles of light. He physically changed in front of her eyes and transmuted into Kimi. She witnessed, fascinated, this atomic transformation. This apparent alteration of being occurred in a microsecond; in our normal time, it was no time at all. Yet, for Marina it was an eternity.

"Each animal," said Kimi, "woven in this carpet, represents a spirit. Some soar, others delve the depths of the underworld. All has its place.

"It is in existence through atomic attraction, be they weaves of woven threads or the harmonic string of stars, dancing in moonbeams over Venice Beach. We meet in a molecular dimension. Now I am dead... Trust Marina... You have the power of love and life."

As fast as this transformation had taken place it reversed. Marina was once more with Tobias, still dressed in his white suit as he re-emerged atomically. He was familiar, like an umbilical cord to another, nearly forgotten existence.

"Are you ready?" he asked.

"Yes," she replied.

It was as if they walked an arc of light. They moved through time and space, unburdened by physical presence. Marina closed her eyes as she felt herself, swirling and whirling through dimensions, landing somewhere unknown.

"We must learn of space from within; in order to understand it without. Be sub-atomic," said Tobias with a smile. Marina sensed herself on the carpet. She closed her eyes clinging to the cloth for she had a sensation of being sucked elsewhere.

In no time at all they were somewhere completely different.

She became aware of a clinical aroma. They had arrived somewhere sterile and full of tensions. As her being adjusted to the situation, things took on a more solid perspective.

She noted everybody, including her and Tobias, were dressed in white gowns. She had a feeling of vitality and significance.

Tobias started speaking. She knew instinctively, they were invisible to everyone else:

"Before a human is born onto the Earth it is full of brightness. It brings its own light to the world, through the tunnel of man into the womb of woman.

"On its journey the extremes of light, joy and happiness or the dark of sadness and aloneness follow. Each can choose which to follow. Why not choose the light?"

"He's not responding. His blood pressure's falling. We've got a problem!"

Several machines beeped a warning.

Marina was distracted by the voices. She saw the surgical tools. The chemicals attached to the body on the bed and the panic of doctors and nurses, unable to save a life.

"Look at your friend," said Tobias.

He pointed at the person on the bed. She studied him further and almost instantly she recognised her friend, Malcolm. He was pale, a ghastly white, barely breathing. She could see his open chest and the beating heart within. There were tubes attached everywhere. The scene clarified further. They were watching an operation.

Marina thought she had gone mad.

"Trust me," resonated Kimi's voice.

"You must kiss his forehead," said Tobias. "No one will see. Do it and we can get out of this place. Come now," he encouraged.

In a trance, Marina walked over. Nobody noticed her. She was in a dimension the living could not see. She bent over. Her lips brushed his forehead. She felt a huge love within. It seemed to transfer, rush from her spirit into his.

The beeping of the machines lessened.

'He's stabilising," she heard a nurse say.

"Time," Tobias stated.

Instantaneously they were gone. Marina felt survival, this time, depended on fixating on an image sewn into the carpet, until the motion, like time, slowed. They reached another destination.

It was a quiet bay.

The waters lapped gently on an unknown Mediterranean shore. Together, Tobias and Marina sat on their carpet looking out to the sea.

"Here we are. The Magic Isle, twenty years ago—"

"Did that just happen?" cut in Marina.

"What has just happened is twenty years later than just now," laughed Tobias.

He looked twenty years younger.

"Nothing is as it seems. Some see differently. Everyone in all eras will say we are solid... If you dispute it... Be you Jesus... Muhammad... Buddha or Krishna... They will prove slavery to the body by destroying the physical presence. But the Spirit survives the death of the body as you witness.

"There are two ways to live life. One as though nothing is miraculous; the other as if all and everything is miraculous. It is insane to keep doing again and again the same things expecting different results. Reality is an illusion that never goes away..."

Marina closed her eyes as she felt the carpet taking them elsewhere.

In the blink of an eye they were back on Carroll Canal, in the capsule-shaped kitchen as if nothing had happened. Tobias, still dressed in his white suit, was mixing drinks:

"As I said: vodka, triple sec, together with crushed ice." He poured the mixture, evenly, into two champagne glasses and then with an explosion uncorked a bottle. It brought

Marina back to Venice Beach with a bang. He passed her a glass, nonchalantly.

"What happened?" she demanded, defiantly.

"Tonight was an initiation," explained Tobias. "Our ceremony for Kimi. She knew her fate before we did and from now you inherit her power. She could heal from a distance. It is the lore not the law. So, in this moment, you chose a life not a death. You chose a friend."

"Are you talking about..." Marina stopped.

She felt overpowered by weariness.

Tobias put his finger to his lips.

"A great woman has been laid to rest today. Her wishes and her will carried out by us. Drink. Now you remember our evening in Maine. All of it I wonder?"

"Not quite," she responded.

On the carpet an image of a golden hare leapt into her sight. It shone in the darkness of night before bouncing off to be transfixed in the face of the moon.

"You may remember something more of our journey. Remember it as a dream."

Tobias turned to her in the dimly lit space; warmth issued from his soul.

"What did your lips last kiss?"

Suddenly Marina was desperately tired.

"Time to get some rest."

She took his outstretched hand and he led her to the bedroom.

21

Malcolm lay, in the recovery room, blissfully unaware of attempting to recover consciousness from surgery. He was attached to various machines that aided his natural functions. His physical body was motionless and inert. To all intents and purposes, Malcolm was perceptually dead to this world. Yet, for the blood to continue to flow, even aided and abetted by the latest innovations, the spirit body must still have a life somewhere, despite the darkness that enveloped its existence.

Where was it?

He did not know, for the spirit was far from its home, within his body. His soul was lost in a molecular ocean so far from that physical self it felt an urge to remain with a light, which had suddenly illuminated the darkness. It lulled him. He felt surrounded by the souls of his ancestors. He could sense their warmth and wanted to merge, be one with them. They were the source, turning shadow to light; calling him, beckoning him and he drifted towards their voices. It was like he had an opportunity to merge with them all.

'Where am I now?' The words flashed into his consciousness.

"Waking the dead and it is not time to stop," responded a man's voice.

"I must face my own death. Not hide on the pick-up truck of tomorrow," he responded defiantly.

"Only love can defy time," he remembered the sweet tones of the speaker. It struck a chord in his now mending heart.

"Come back with us," she murmured.

He saw a tunnel of light. It stretched down from some vague part of the solar system, where his spirit self had wandered, to his hospital bed. In an instant he was following the lighted pathway that reunited his body and soul. Nothing was solid. All manifested as atomic in structure. He sensed two people in a chair.

One of them was speaking:

"So, one moment here, next moment gone; did the space ship pick you up, as you said it would? Cos one moment here, next moment frozen in an icy stare, gone elsewhere." It was Tobias.

"You know the molecules of the body and the molecules of the mind were made up long ago in the furnace of an ancient star burning in the heavens." The sweet tone was Marina's.

"The Earth is in a critical condition. Daily the crisis increases. We need radical change in our culture. Our untapped intuitive and psychic forces that we need to survive are forces society programmes us to disregard. You must help stop it," added Tobias.

Malcolm had an alien feeling. He heard his breathing. Consciousness was returning. He slowly started to feel pain. There seemed to be tubes everywhere. The sensation of two of these tubes in his stomach was very odd. He could feel his arms tingling. His eyelids fluttered.

The bodies speaking to him were taking form. Recognition and thought, apparently, woke up.

'It is Tobias and Marina,' he deduced, before his eyes closed again and he seemed to float towards the stars once more.

He was transported back in time to when he was six. Together with his mother, he had travelled to the west coast of Ireland to visit her father, his grandfather, in County Mayo. The contrast between the compactness of the countryside of Ireland, compared to the vastness of his home in California, was overwhelming. His grandfather was a small man with sparkling eyes. He lived in a white, thatched cottage. His mother left them together when she went out, which was often.

He would tell tales to Malcolm that conjured up magical, strange images. He seemed to weave timeless stories that fascinated Malcolm and took him to spaces no television or computer could reveal.

In a month they were best friends. As he lay in his hospital bed, time and the years dissolved. He was, once more, in the cottage sitting room, listening to the old man:

"So, perhaps," his grandfather concluded, "we think this life is complete in itself? But maybe God didn't make it so easy. Perhaps it is just a starting point and death is just a bigger birth?" He grinned.

It was an image forever etched on Malcolm's mind. The grin remained on his grandfather's face as he exhaled and never inhaled again. These were his final words spoken on this earth. Malcolm was back in the room, as he had been that day, alone with a dead man, silently awaiting the return of his mother to discover them and for him to break down in tears of anguish.

"Love defies time; it is not time for you," he heard Marina whisper.

In a flash he was back in his body. He watched her get up with Tobias to leave. As she passed him, he felt her lips brush his forehead. It reminded him of something. He felt a surge of energy. His eyelids fluttered again. There was a stabbing pain in his stomach and he groaned.

"Malcolm?" He heard a female voice and it was not Marina's. He felt disappointed.

"Is he coming around?" said someone else.

His eyes opened, and the atomic structure began to take on a normal, solid form.

"I'll tell the doctor." Malcolm recognised the speaker. It was Mark, his fellow lecturer, whom he last saw at the art gallery.

Soon a doctor in a white coat stood in front of him asking him some questions. He was weary but replied competently.

"You've had a new aortic valve transplant and you're very lucky to be alive. You get seventy-two hours observation here then home. Give it a month you'll be as right as rain," the doctor said brightly.

"Hang on how did I get here? What happened?" asked Malcolm.

As he'd regained consciousness and the body and spirit merged, his unconscious journey started to fade, as the reality of his wakening state hit home.

"The last thing I remember," he said weakly, "was getting out of bed." He recalled the taste in his mouth.

"But you sent me a message. Telling me to come over. I came over. The door was open. You were collapsed in your bedroom. It's weird. How do you pass out and then open the door? How did you send me a text message?"

The woman's voice was high-pitched and slightly hysterical.

"You just don't remember," she cried. "Remember me, Phoebe, of Junk Joy and Jung? Hey, I called you a jerk but I saved your life."

"I think that's enough for now, you had better go," interrupted the doctor, to Malcolm's relief. He had tried to look at Phoebe, but it just gave him a pain in the neck.

"I'm going to increase the pain killers. You need more rest," said the doctor adjusting one of the attachments to his arm. "Don't worry you'll be okay. You've been lucky."

Malcolm smiled. He felt the pain lessen and started to calm down. He tried to assimilate what he remembered, but it became hazy. For some reason that he could not understand, the image of Marina and Tobias filled his mind, before he slowly and gently slipped into sleep.

Simultaneously, on Carroll Canal, in Venice Beach, Marina, once more awoke alone. Her head was throbbing with pain. She got up to find the house was small and dingy, nothing like her memory of the previous night. It had a cold, stale atmosphere. She made coffee and decided to take it in the garden.

As she passed the lounge she glanced inside. It looked completely undisturbed, as if no one had been there for ages.

'Beep…Beep…' insisted her phone, breaking into her mental wanderings.

She stared into the room again and realised, incredulously, there was no carpet, of any shape or size, to be seen.

22

Suzann awoke wrapped in satin sheets. She took a deep, satisfied breath, closed her eyes and recalled the journey from Venice, to Frank's house in the Hollywood Hills.

She remembered how, as the car had climbed the road, she was captivated by the glittering city below, sparkling in an array of dazzling, electric illuminations.

It made her feel wild. She wanted to let go. Suzann blushed at the memory.

She recalled, clearly, how the night had unfolded and her nakedness, as she awoke only added to her sense of embarrassment. She remembered them entering his opulent mansion. She liked his naïve pride and innocent demeanour. They drank champagne together, overlooking that city of angels beneath the full moon. Suzann had been enchanted.

She remembered sensing a plea – had it been Marina or Malcolm?

It was a moment made to be forgotten, followed by a hallucinated vision of Kimi. Suzann spotted her image standing on the 'Y' of the Hollywood sign. Once seen, in a flash, leaving a sparkling trail of disappearing stars, Kimi flew to Suzann, whispering:

"Forget Malcolm, Marina and Tobias. The part they play in your life. Right now, forget them. Just be. It's the best you can do."

Kimi disappeared into the trail of stardust she had created. The strange, brief visitation served as a potion for amnesia. Temporarily, Suzann's present past was erased. She moved closer to Frank, taken by the unique ambience and atmosphere of the Hollywood Hills penetrating her being.

She became, seductive and tempting as she drew him into her web. She knew, despite his apparent wealth and fame, that he was just another lonely man, in a mansion, he didn't need. He wanted to share himself.

Suzann mesmerised Frank with her soft, seductive eyes. He melted, entranced by her sensuality and, overwhelmed by desire, he touched her face, gently, caressing her lips. Suddenly Suzann stopped her reflections.

She was wide-awake and didn't dare recall what happened next. She heard footsteps. They distracted her and took her mind away from the events of last night. She could smell the coffee.

She snuggled down into the bed, closed her eyes and pretended to be asleep.

"Hey, my little sorceress," Frank greeted her hidden body.

"I'm taking my coffee onto the terrace," he added softly. "I've put a gown at the end of the bed. It's for you. Join me. You're beautiful," he concluded, and she heard him walk off.

She smiled at his final statement. It showed how he had enjoyed her. She had enjoyed him as well. She felt her cheeks redden again. It was a trifle she could easily forget.

For a moment she was troubled by the thought of her husband, but she knew of several of his dalliances, so felt no guilt and decided to revel in the experience. She got out of bed, slipped on the gown and joined Frank on the terrace.

"Hey," he got up and held her.

She kissed him lightly, withdrew and took a seat.

"Coffee?" he asked, adding:

"L.A. is 469 square miles. Look out there you can see it all just about. The Valley, Westwood, downtown, San Bernardino, Santa Monica – it's all there, spread out before the eyes. A city where they make dreams."

"It's an amazing sight Frank. Thank you so much," replied Suzann in a gentle, appreciative tone. She sipped the coffee he gave her.

"I've been offered a new part; a true story about some weird English poet." Frank paused and put on his actor's persona, as he quoted:

"Hush... Be still... Outer space is a concept not a place. Try no more. Where we are; never can be sky or star. From prison in a prison we fly. There is no way into the sky!"

He paused, stopped quoting then continued in his normal voice:

"What is this guy trying to say? I don't get it. Not sure I can do this; it's a real challenge. Kimi would have advised me. Sorry I'm speaking because I want to be with you."

Suzann was disturbed by the tone of his last statement. It was not acting.

"Frank, you did that very well. There's something about you deeper than that detective you play. Lighten up. I have to go and may never see you again."

"You'll miss me," he predicted.

She let her robe momentarily slip before gathering it in.

"I must take a shower."

Frank smiled.

"When you're ready we can leave together. I've got the limo till the end of the week. We can stop on Rodeo drive. I can take you to the airport later? Whatever you want."

"You don't have to. I'll think about it as I get ready," Suzann said. She went inside.

Thirty minutes later she reappeared:

"I'll need a new dress," she smiled shyly.

"You know Suzann, I don't get attached. You're going back to New York, to a husband and I want to be attached to you. Why do I want what I can never have?"

He was close to her. His eyes were like doors into his soul and Suzann glimpsed inside, before the portal closed on his openness. She felt a wave of emotion towards him.

"Maybe I should call Marina?" The question instantly altered the ambience.

She walked to the terrace for privacy. Already she realised there was a problem with Frank. He was too attached to her and she could sense it. Nevertheless, she consoled herself with the thought that once back in Manhattan, this would all be just a memory.

Looking out over the hills, Suzann dialled Marina:

"All well?" she asked.

"Not so sure. Cab has just arrived to take me to the hotel. Can you meet me there? By the way have you heard anything from Malcolm?"

"No. Why?" Suzann felt an anxiety in her tone.

"Where are you?" asked Marina.

"Just about to leave the Hollywood Hills. I'll be with you as soon as I can."

Suzann put the phone down and once more looked out at the landscape. It was the first time she noticed the red rim of pollution, trapped in the basin where the city was built. She sensed last night fade, as the larger picture of her life came back into perspective.

"Okay," she said to Frank.

"Sure, but first." He held her tightly looking in her eyes and kissed her long and deeply, on the lips.

"A reminder," he whispered.

"You won't forget me," she responded with surety.

"Come on," she added and together, they walked out into the L.A. sunshine.

23

Over a month after Malcolm's surgery, Tobias appeared to flit through the crowds on 42nd street, making his way downtown. He appeared a large man, slightly portly, but not overweight in terms of physical stature. He had a generosity of spirit, which, combined with his customary white djellaba and multi-coloured Kashmiri cap, seemed to magnetise others, wherever he found himself in the world.

His type belonged to a rare tradition going back thousands of years. Born to travel an internal journey, regardless of the social scenario they lived through, be it gladiators or footballers, it made no difference to their doom. There was something ghost like and ethereal in Tobias's gait, as he seamlessly made his way through the crowds, up towards the east side of Central Park.

Malcolm was in his downtown loft apartment.

Since his operation, life had altered drastically, for him. His value system had fundamentally changed. Once he started recovering, the reason why he'd been saved was not only a mystery to him, but also a constant, unanswered, question. Everyone sympathised with his plight. However, they were unable to understand the mental scars left by such a physical trauma. One doctor joked how:

"The body doesn't know the difference between open heart surgery and being torn apart by a sabre-toothed tiger." The metaphor stuck in his head.

Malcolm was mystified by his own spiritual transformation. Several unanswered questions kept recurring in his mind. How, that morning, did he make the call to Phoebe? How could he have opened a door in a state of unconsciousness? It defied logic.

Now, nearly back to normal, he contemplated a return to work as his friends had encouraged him to do. He was dubious about how he would deal with it, purely because since his physical crisis, psychology had taken on a superficial, almost meaningless role. He felt it misled people.

The doorbell rang and interrupted his musings. Usually he ignored any unexpected interruptions but for some reason, with a sense of anticipation, he decided to answer.

It was Tobias.

"Wow, man. Great to see you! I was passing. Aren't you going to invite me in? We've had enough digital calls. Time for a one-to-one and I like the apartment," he remarked, walking through the open door. He sat comfortably in a chair.

Malcolm was shocked. He hadn't seen Tobias since Maine.

"Have you visited Marina?" he asked.

"No and I won't but do tell her I dropped in," responded Tobias.

"What?" asked Malcolm.

"Ha," laughed Tobias. "Do not meddle in the affairs of wizards for they are subtle and quick to anger. I think Mister Tolkien said that or was it Gandalf? But seriously, does she visit you?"

"Yes, she does," Malcolm, replied. "I'm not sure that without her…"

Tobias cut in and completed his question:

"You would have survived?"

"What is about you?" Malcolm was irked by the sarcasm in Tobias's comment.

"I don't understand," he continued angrily. "One moment you are here, next moment gone. I'm not sure what happens with you, but you are out of my realm and Marina's."

He paused, then carried on in a conciliatory fashion:

"I'm sorry. Really, I should be thanking you. Somehow, you're partly to blame for me still being alive. I have an illogical sense that's the case. I'm not sure whether to resent it or bless it."

There was a brief silence. The atmosphere between them seemed to intensify. Tobias spoke softly:

"Well I came to find out if Marina was all right. I can see she is in good hands—" he paused, and the silence intensified before he continued, obscurely:

"What is born must die. What is reaped will be dispensed and exhausted. All that is built up is destined to collapse. All that is high will be brought low. We need to be allies not friends."

"What do you mean?"

"I mean we are on the same side, part of an unfolding fate. Do one thing infinitesimally different and tomorrow will be infinitely different. For millennia the universe speaks to us in gravitational waves. It arrives, reaching us from light years away. We are deaf to the resonance. We hear only the heartbeat of our own ego. Your heart beats on but for each life there is a death."

"Why not visit Marina?" Malcolm suggested. "She told me about Venice Beach."

Tobias replied, again at a tangent:

"People are afraid of death because they do not know who they are. Everyone is obsessed with believing in their own fantasy of themselves. What they consider to be their identity. If you examine that identity, or ego, it disintegrates because it is made entirely of things external to a person. Their name, age, partner, underwear, family, dress, home, job, friends; these all define who they are. It is an appearance, an image, which, when stripped away, leaves a person empty and with no idea of who they are. Once the outer self is exposed to the inner universe, the real journey begins."

"I'm, maybe, just getting a sense of that," mused Malcolm.

"Everyone is different. For instance, with Marina, what she remembers is only what she is able to. I can tell her no more. If I speak to her now, all she will want is for me to answer questions she should not have the answers to. It is better I stay away."

For a moment everything changed.

The proportions of the room distorted. Objects turned into bizarre, irregular shapes. The walls began morphing with mesmerising colours. The solidity began disintegrating into an atomic dimension and Malcolm was witnessing it. He was reminded of waking up after his operation. It happened in a flash, before all returned to normality.

"It's not your heart," remarked Tobias.

Malcolm sensed he knew what had just taken place.

"She must have changed since she came back from Los Angeles, Marina that is. Maybe Suzann too," mused Tobias.

"I'd been here, maybe three days when they first came and visited," replied Malcolm. "Suzann couldn't stay long but Marina did. After that she's been here at least twice a week. In fact, she's the only person I see, who I can tolerate. The only one I look forward to seeing. Everyone else just makes me angry." Malcolm stopped.

"My way is not your way, yet we are inter-connected. I am not as you see me, like the walls of this room," stated Tobias. He stood up. The ambience lightened. He opened his arms to be hugged and Malcolm embraced him.

"I gotta go man."

"Already?"

"I've said what I have to say; make of it what you will. Give my best to Suzann and Marina."

For a big man, Tobias was surprisingly light on his feet. He didn't waste time and without further ado, quickly and almost invisibly, he disappeared from the apartment.

Malcolm scratched his head.

"Did that really happen?" he said out loud.

"Beep… Beep," replied his phone and any further contemplation of Tobias's visit, became subjugated to the insistent demands of modern technology.

24

Marina looked out of her apartment window, west, across Central Park. Before her was not the phantasmagoria and wonder of the Manhattan architecture, but the last month of her life. Her eyes were red from tears. In her right hand she clutched a letter she'd been reading.

She remembered returning from California. How she threw herself headlong back into her habitual Manhattan lifestyle. It made her feel secure, despite the risks and high stakes involved in the financial markets. She complained and resented how her life was structured. It was dominated by her work, but deep down she didn't want to change it.

It gave her a thrill to gamble and it was safe gambling money. In the world of Tobias, she felt out of her depth. Her refuge, as it had been in Maine, was work. She remembered too clearly what happened on Carroll Canal. It scared her.

As she looked across the landscape, bedazzled by the varying vibrancies of the city, she realised how she used her powers of seeing to bewitch men. Each male conquest was a testimony to her continuing attractiveness. It was an asset she used so much it had become almost instinctive. Manipulating men with her sensuality and denying any responsibility gave her satisfaction.

She knew what she was doing, even if her victim had no idea. It was an uncomfortable thought to accept but she was vulnerable, emotionally opened, by the contents of the letter in her hand.

After California she had wanted to feel safe. She did this by throwing herself into familiar world of outer elegance. The deeper, invisible world of esotericism was subjugated to her search for material comfort. The Yankee dollar beckoned more than the understanding she craved.

It was carved into the rocks of Central Park, the flashing advertising signs near 57th street and the gargoyles of the Dakota building. She was conscious of a sweeping emotion, the same feeling she had felt during her experience with Tobias in Venice. It moved like a wave of traffic on Park Avenue.

She swayed and gripped the letter tighter in her hand. She was anxious, uncertain as the clouds that raced over the dark, night sky.

Only several hours earlier she went to visit Malcolm. She envisaged the meeting still staring at the metropolis beneath her.

It was difficult to fit Malcolm in to her schedule. She resented it. Then she felt the reverse emotion – a feeling that her presence helped him. In return, it opened something for her. The afternoon's conversation came back to her word for word, written in the stars above her.

"Maybe all of this matters no more. The heartbeat and the breath I am finally beaten into submission. Ouch." Malcolm winced. "I've been going through some of Tobias's papers. Like to hear what he's written?"

"Sure."

"Ok," Malcolm began. He swept his hair back and, theatrically as he could under the circumstances, read:

"What is this ache? This watered-down version of love, eating the life out of me? We start innocently but end up a mass of contradictions."

He paused and changed his delivery:

"She is in a cage of her own making, imprisoned and confined by habit. Snapping, biting and snarling at freedom from suffering. Habit, habit, habit, figures, numbers, money."

Then in a different voice:

"Should I have not been a man? Pretended, instead, to be an enchanted eunuch? At your beck and call? I may never love again. Thank you for reminding me I still have a heart to be broken!"

"I like that, it's funny," giggled Malcolm, "and one more he quoted:

"Her whole life was spent making men want her. Why would I be different? Her success is my failure."

Malcolm closed the notebook.

"It's quite mysterious. Tobias is quite mysterious," observed Malcolm. "And there is definitely something romantic and self-effacing about him. But he's more ghost-like than human. Each moment is a life and death in itself. No one realises it until it is too late. Imagine how the daybreak, the sunrise would look, on your day of execution? Brighter than ever...

"Marina, your presence helps me. You should trust in your instinct and where it takes you. What you are doing, working with money, is no longer a challenge."

"I hate what I'm doing," she admitted.

In her vision over Central Park, as she recollected the conversation with Malcolm, tears distorted her sight. They trickled down her cheeks as she recollected the scene:

"You don't understand. Every day I work fourteen hours. I must think and act to take care of tomorrow. Sometimes I work so late. There is a young man; he helps when I am tired. He will do anything for me. He is like a lap dog. Maybe I can heal but it is a world I do not know. I prefer to suffer by breaking men's hearts than to gamble on destiny. Maybe if out of the blue, I no longer needed to worry about money. I'd be forced to explore another direction. It will not happen."

She remembered smiling and wiping her tears.

The conversation faded before the night landscape and turned the streets into a revelation of her life. They took on a form of almost robotically-governed screens, flashing financial numbers. She was emblazoned on the wall of a building or amusing herself with playful flirtations. She was in despair at her automatism, for she recognised how mechanical her reactions had become.

It was then she turned away from the window and went inside. She sat down and with a sigh, once more read the letter in her hand:

'Dear Marina,

By the time you read this letter I will be dead. I asked the lawyer to wait before sending it. I have left you a considerable sum of money. It is more than enough for you not to work again.

You must learn to accept love and give it, wholly, not just at your convenience. Become a healer. To get another person to gamble their heart on you, or gamble on anything outside, is easy. Gamble on your spirit to show you an unimaginable way. There is only one game and that's the game of life.

My love to you.'

Marina put down the letter. She knew, just from the day's events she had no choice. Her fate was sealed.

25

Suzann smoothed her dress and stared at her reflection in the mirror. She inhaled, feeling the air in her lungs, holding it and counting to ten, before exhaling as deeply as she had taken the breath in. The effects of her earlier yoga class were still coursing through her.

Nevertheless, it did little to silence her emotional turmoil, which had increased considerably since she came back from California. Her night with Frank lingered. His voice and presence always haunted her, whatever the situation.

"You seem distracted, somewhere else," Paul had observed the previous night.

"And how would you know?" She had responded. It reminded him of how little time they spent together.

She remembered the conversation as she, absent-mindedly rearranged some flowers in one of the vases.

Her marriage, she reflected, was mutually beneficial and socially enhancing. It looked good, even though the passion had run its course, while inside, in terms of their views of the world, they were living on different planets. She looked around their beautifully-designed apartment. Her doorbell rang. It was Marina.

"So glad to see you," she welcomed. They hugged each other and went inside.

"Okay, phones off," suggested Marina. "We need to talk without wondering who might interrupt us."

"Are you all right Marina? A visit in the middle of the week and in the daytime, it's a first! Let's go in the kitchen and I'll make some tea."

In Suzann's apartment, out of the kitchen window, the view took in the East River, Roosevelt Island and distant Queens. It was a stupendous sight. Especially when you were warm indoors on a winter's day looking out at that man-made maze, beneath a blue sky shrouded by white racing, oblique, clouds.

"So, what is it?" asked Suzann.

"I've resigned."

"What? How will you survive?"

"A week ago, I was talking with Malcolm. He's become like Tobias, telling me I'm wasted in the world of finance. If I had enough money I wouldn't work with money as the major motivation. Why would I? As a joke I promised as I left that if I ever became financially secure I'd stop work immediately. I'd develop something different. Find a way to live, which combined what I want to do with my survival. I went home that night. There was a letter on the floor. It was from Kimi's lawyer. She's left me enough money to do exactly what I'd been saying at Malcolm's earlier.

Suzann felt a fluttering in her stomach. She kept her emotional self well under control. Yet Marina's revelation caused an unexpected envy. She wanted to burst into tears for her reaction was jealousy, rather than delight. She didn't show it in her words:

"It's wonderful, Marina. Go on," she encouraged.

"You're the first I've spoken about it with. I still have to clear up some things and hand them over. It's the first day, today, in my life I haven't had a job or worried about survival. I now realise that at work I am dirty inside and I compensate by making the outside appear polished and clean. Perhaps now, inside myself, I can let go of the dirt gathered over the decades."

The atmosphere between them deepened. Suzann listened intently:

"No one can buy back time. I played on men's desire, a woman's greatest weapon for success, in a man's world. I had no choice. I used my femininity but maybe, now, I can explore it more deeply? Maybe my physical attraction reflects an inner state? The body dies but what of the spirit?"

Suzann got up and walked to the window. She looked at the buzzing, dashing city below meditatively and began:

"Funny how we are so opposite," she mused, returning to her seat.

"For you, suddenly all is open. For me it's closing time. My whole security is under threat. Why? What was the catalyst? The same as yours and I am so happy for you Marina. For me the dream has turned into a nightmare."

Suzann stopped. She put her head in her hands.

Marina walked over and put her arm round her friend:

"Hey. It's okay. Tell me," soothed Marina.

"The night with Frank. I never felt freer. I wanted to keep it like that. A precious memory of a precious time; I'm pregnant."

With the admission she sobbed uncontrollably. Everything she had built in life was threatened by a moment of passion and love. Her sobs subsided, and she pulled herself together. She kissed Marina:

"I'm sorry. I had to tell someone. Can you get a tissue?" she asked. "I needed that," she added, wiping away her tears. "I must have an abortion."

"You can't do that," responded Marina.

Suzann stood up, her face reddened, her voice angry.

"I can't believe you said that. Two weeks ago, you'd be finding me a doctor. What about my marriage? All this?" She swept her arms around the room:

"Look this is my life and security. It's under threat. What would I do if I had this child? Huh? What would you do without your sudden legacy? Let a pregnancy ruin the games you play to make money? No." There was contempt and bitterness in Suzann's tone.

Marina sat quietly. She felt composed. Something insisted she remain calm.

Suzann sat down again, head in hands before sitting straight up again:

"I'm sorry to say it, but it is true isn't it?" she said.

"Yes," agreed Marina. She waited a moment then began speaking again. The words she spoke seemed to come from another part of her being:

"You do not need to be ashamed. We may not be particularly enlightened, peaceful or clever. Nevertheless, we

133

are soil good enough to cultivate. What is planted in us, we can do nothing about. You are a warrior too. You're not cheating anybody nor want to. Frank, me, Paul, an unborn child, maybe it is supposed to be.

"Tomorrow is a fantasy. Right now, your vision is not a beautiful setting-sun vision. A seed has been planted in you. It is very simple and straightforward. To me, it is very beautiful what has happened. There is the gift of life inside you. It is a legacy richer than money. Keep that in your vision of the future."

Marina's words calmed Suzann. She felt unburdened and her desperation faded. Since realising her symptoms were a result of her pregnancy, her mind had only thought of termination. Now, for the first time, she contemplated an alternative.

"I will help you Suzann, in whatever way I can. Whatever you decide," added Marina.

"It's another few weeks before I have to decide. Just for you I'll think about all the options," Suzann managed a rueful laugh. Her spirits had been lifted.

Marina sensed an opportunity:

"Let's go out. Have some lunch, why not? Get you out of the house. We have the whole day together in front of us. Come on." Her enthusiasm was infectious.

"Okay," agreed Suzann, getting up, smoothing her dress and stretching. They put on their coats and walked to the door.

"One other thing. You should text Frank and tell him," advised Marina.

"I'll think about it," replied Suzann.

26

One week later, Frank was attending the premiere of a science fiction film, entitled 'Saturn and Satan'. He played the commander, of an alien force, allied to human attempts at colonising the stars. It was a big budget movie and his agent had assured him it was a great career move.

He had played his part well. He was at the party after the 'first showing'. He was smiling, stopping to accept congratulations from acquaintances and people he hardly knew. Although with each glass of champagne, the glitterati and sparkling positivity of the production combined to have him fantasising about an acceptance speech for an Oscar.

He chuckled at the thought of impending success. As he strolled round the room, his vanity encouraged, he congratulated himself on how he had achieved material stability. It was time, he thought, to work on his personal life.

"Hey, Frank. I can't believe it. My second ex-husband is here. You don't mind. He's invited me to a party in Beverley Hills. I think I'll go," said Janet, who accompanied him to the event.

"No problem, go ahead, take the limo" he replied with relief and kissed her as if he would miss her.

"You are such a gentleman," she whispered.

He was happy to see her disappear into the crowd. He didn't really like her, but he needed to be seen with someone. It didn't matter now. He knew from these affairs, an hour after these parties began they were more or less over, as people's indulgences took control.

He was grateful to be alone. He decided to leave the main room and go outside. He walked into the, warm, balmy, Westwood air and felt a relief at finding some space away from people.

He took a seat by the pool and looked at the stars. A waiter came by and filled his glass. He drank it absent-mindedly. His thoughts wandered far from the science fiction fantasy film and his performance. The world of Hollywood 'make-believe' dissolved as, once more, the text he received from Suzann earlier, flashed like a neon sign over his consciousness:

"I'm pregnant. There is only one possible father and that's you. Someone advised me to share with you. It was a fling, a beautiful moment to be terminated."

The acting skills displayed in the film his contemporaries complimented him on were nothing compared to his performance that night. In reality, he was in a state of shock. He felt a mixture of love and contempt for Suzann, as earlier he smiled and nodded, or spoke politely about cinema.

The apprehension, the excitement of fatherhood, such an unexpected possibility, stood before him, but the tone of Suzann implied the child's survival would have nothing to do with him.

He dialled her number yet again and got the same machine answer. He swore under his breath. He was angry, and the champagne had not helped; also, who could he talk to?

'No one.' He sighed, got up and in the shadows bumped into a passing figure.

"Watch where you're going," Frank said aggressively.

"Cool it man," responded the figure.

There was something vaguely familiar about him.

"Do I know you from somewhere?"

"Wow! Yes. Aren't you Suzann's friend? It is you. I cannot believe it. Sit down please. I remember I saw you briefly at the funeral. You're Tobias. What are you doing here?"

"Same as you, escaping the crowd," replied Tobias joining him.

"And I'm thinking of Suzann," Frank replied.

"Ah! The rose in bloom," remarked Tobias.

"What do you mean?"

"Exactly that."

"So, you know as well?"

"Should a rose be plucked? Or left on the branch? In what way do birth and death intermingle and make a bridge?"

"Man, you are obscure. I don't understand you, but my guess is you know Suzann is pregnant."

"And you're the father," finished Tobias with a chuckle.

"It's not funny," slurred Frank.

He was drunk enough to be veering towards aggression.

"What would you like? A boy or a girl?" asked Tobias tenderly.

"Little girl," dreamed Frank. "But Suzann wants an abortion."

"So, life and death again. If they were both so simple."

"Life isn't but death is."

"Do we know?" asked Tobias leaning forward.

"Maybe there is more much more. Layers, strata, worlds within worlds spinning in a vortex. Throughout the ages people believed, and still do, in the spirit between worlds, who can appear to some and not to others. It is another space to the outer space in your movie."

"I don't understand you. In fact, I can't follow. Maybe it's the champagne."

"You're a young spirit, Frank and there are plenty of places for you to be, alive or dead."

"But I want life," Frank exclaimed. "Look at it."

He stood up, pointing at the heavens before slumping back into his seat.

"She should have my baby, my child. I'd marry her," Frank demanded of the invisible. He received no response and broke down momentarily.

"I'd do anything for her", he continued, almost pleading, "for her to have that child. I'd give anything. Even my life."

As he spoke he felt a power rush through him, as if his wish meant more than he bargained for. It didn't last. He covered his face:

"She won't listen to me," he despaired.

"Be calm Frank. I'll speak to her. All is as it should be. Life is ahead of us and it is already done. A child or no child you cannot argue with what is. Never pretend to a love, which you do not actually feel. Love is not ours to command. Everything is a circle. I admire your courage."

"My courage? For what?"

"For saying you would give life for your unborn child. It's admirable."

Tobias' words calmed Frank. His inner rage subsided.

"You're a strange man, Tobias. Suzann and Kimi spoke about you. I know of you, more from others' discussions, than any personal experience. The thing is, are you a lucky charm or an evil eye, a man of vision or just a vision? Why did that go through my mind?" Frank observed obliquely.

Tobias responded:

"Think of the film we have just watched. One of the reasons we go to the cinema, is that, as we watch, we forget our own past and future. We are absorbed, taken from the constant conflict with ourselves, and how we manifest.

"We live in an eternal now, fantasising pasts and futures. But as we watch a film, our so-important past and future, ceases to exist. We are absorbed by the now, of a man-made fantasy."

"I'm not a deep man, Tobias. I never was. I'm a Midwest boy who made good, except when it came to love. I look back, I see my mom. She would be proud. I look forward and I'm anxious. Now all I see is Suzann and my child inside her," he paused and looked up at the billions of points of light pulsating in the sky.

"I'm tiny; my life is nothing," he concluded.

It was getting late. More people had stepped out from the main hall into the outside area and the bar by the pool where Frank and Tobias sat. A couple passed by and stopped.

The girl, in her mid-twenties, wore a short, skimpy black dress, black tights and dark rouge lipstick. The man wore an hombre hat with feathers. His shirt was open to reveal his necklaces tumbling over his hairy chest.

"My God! It's Frank Whitely!" The girl stopped, awestruck.

"Oh man," her companion interrupted. "That scene in the film where that guy on Saturn's third moon tells you he's dead but he's like a normal person and you go…Like… Yea and you say like…" He held his arms, as if aiming a rifle.

The girl put her hands on the table and her face close to Frank's as she finished off the tale:

"You think you're dead but alive? I'll show you and you zap him with your laser and he disappears into one of those rings." She leaned forward and kissed him full on the lips. Her companion pulled her off:

"Hey leave him, honey. Come on," and they vanished into the shadows.

"I'm sorry," said Frank and turned to Tobias.

The chair was empty. He was alone. He tried to work out how, unnoticed, Tobias had slipped away. But as he thought the thought, Tobias seemed to come out of nowhere, carrying two full champagne glasses.

"One for the road," he said. "All those fans. It is a great scene in the film how you zap the living dead. But let me tell you something. He leaned forward:

"We live in a culture completely hypnotised by illusions. It enables the so-called present moment to be subjugated, felt to be nothing compared to our all-powerful past and important future. We have no present. Our consciousness is almost completely preoccupied with memory and expectation.

"Zap it with a laser beam like this present experience. We are out of touch with reality. The world as talked about, described, and measured, like the girl who just kissed you. Social conveniences, like money, are absurd and not to be taken seriously and confused with real wealth.

"In some ways, thoughts, ideas and words are 'coins', means of exchange. What is rare is valuable. We all must pay the Ferryman!"

Tobias laughed and drank his champagne.

Frank nodded his head. He felt unburdened and although Suzann remained in his mind, his feelings of anxiety and desperation to speak to her subsided.

The sense Tobias gave, of there being little one can do about where one finds oneself in life, had calmed him.

"Even in death there may be life," Frank commented.

"And maybe the dead walk in life?" smiled Tobias.

"Then I'd zap them with my laser! Boom."

Frank stood up as if he was shooting Tobias, who fell down pretending death, before getting up ghoulishly and laughing.

Frank felt dizzy and started swaying, Tobias put his arm round him.

"Hey. You need help to get a cab, man! Come on pull yourself together!" he ordered.

Frank put on a reasonably steady face and they went to the foyer.

"The ex," he slurred, "took the limo. Guess I have to stand in line."

"No problem," said Tobias and stayed with him till he was safely in the back of a cab.

"Sure you don't want a lift. You can stay?" invited Frank.

"No. There's someone meeting me here, in half an hour. But it's been a great meeting," Tobias shook his hand.

"Sure has. What's that?" Said Frank opening the hand Tobias had just shaken. It contained a silver dollar.

"A memento for your performance," explained Tobias.

"Or a coin to pay that Ferryman you were talking about?" laughed Frank.

Tobias watched as the cab drove off. He smiled and held his arms out, as if play acting the part of Frank, zapping the living dead, in the movie.

Tobias perceived a larger canvas and understood the consequences. His atomic structure's speed of materialisation was faster than others. It put him in another dimension.

Meanwhile, on a whim, Frank told the driver to take him to West Hollywood. He wanted another drink, in a sleazy bar he knew.

"One for the road and wait for me. I'll make it worth your while," he said, flashing some notes.

"Bit of a weird area Sir, but sure, I'll take and wait as they say."

Frank had no idea that this decision would prove so fortuitous for the success of 'Saturn and Satan'. The legendary status of the film would be woven around the chaotic events of the next and final half hour of his life.

Little did he know that his dream of winning an Oscar was about to become a posthumous reality.

27

Frank felt like a man possessed as they made the short journey to Pete's Bar, which was situated in the Santa Monica Boulevard/-La Brea area. He felt like some sleaze. The moment he left Tobias, it swept over him. It was his revenge. If a woman made him mad, he wanted to beat her.

Pete's Bar specialised in providing this form of sadism. He hadn't been there for some time, but he was determined. The understanding he felt with Tobias was out of the window. They reached his destination.

"I'm going to be about an hour OK, kid?" He flashed a hundred-dollar bill in front of him.

"You want me to wait an hour *here*?" said the young cabbie, incredulously.

"No problem," there was an edge, an aggression to his demand. "Make sure you stay, Alvin." Frank added reading his name tag.

"Don't worry I'll be here." replied Alvin, nervously. It was dark and the boulevard empty.

Frank got out of the car and crossed the street towards Pete's, but he didn't get there. Out of the shadows three men appeared.

"What the fuck?" said one of them on seeing Frank.

"He's got dollars like anyone who wears a dickey bow."

Frank realised how much he must stand out even in the dark but he felt invulnerable. He responded.

"Think I'm a wimp? Think you can do what you want huh?"

"No man. But you've got money for sure and I'm taking it off you." He moved closer. "Are you gonna give it or will we take it? One way or the other we are going to get it."

"Oh yeah? I will zap you with my laser." Frank moved his arm to his inside pocket, but it was a fatal mistake. They believed him.

Two shots split the night air. Frank looked surprised, shocked even. He felt his legs giving way. He didn't understand why. Then there was blackness.

The robbers searched his pockets. They took anything of value, before running into the night.

Alvin had dived beneath the dashboard at the first shot. Once it was silent he looked up. When he was certain they had gone, he got out the cab. He saw Frank lying on the ground. He went over to see how he was.

His open staring, lifeless eyes told their own story.

Frank was dead.

Marina and Suzann were about to leave to terminate her pregnancy when their phones beeped simultaneously. It was an unexpected message from Tobias which, out of the blue suggested:

"Important. Stop whatever you are doing. Watch Fox News."

They looked at each other. Suzann switched on the digital set.

"So, Joe, can you summarise this mystery for us coming out of Hollywood?"

"As best I can Marie. It seems Frank Whitely, best known for his TV showing in 'San Diego Detectives' had been out to the premier of his first movie. He has a major supporting role in Universal's latest potential blockbuster 'Saturn and Satan.'"

"Wow, he was a player," responded Marie.

"Sure was, Marie. It seems he left and went to a bar in West Hollywood."

"Sorry to interrupt Joe but I understand that Jill has an interview with his cab driver."

The TV cut to Alvin the cabbie, chewing gum, making the most of his moment of fame.

"Yeah. I thought it odd he'd go down to that part of town. Still, he's paying. He got out the car, crossed the road. I saw three guys appear. I knew they were up to no good. I heard them arguing. I hid like there was no one in my car. All I could see was someone lying on the ground. I ran over. It was Frank, and he'd been shot dead."

"Hang on. Sorry Joe I've got to interrupt as news is coming in."

Suzann switched off the television. She sat down and put her hands in her head and sobbed. Marina went and comforted her.

"I can't believe it. All that remains living of Frank is inside me." Suzann was verging on hysteria.

Marina was shocked. Only moments ago, she was reluctantly planning to help Suzann terminate her pregnancy. Now the father was dead. It changed everything. Her first concern was Suzann. Marina held her till she calmed down. She sensed her vulnerability and despair.

Suzann was remembering her night in California with Frank. The freedom she felt. There was no denying it. Maybe she hadn't been in love and yet, maybe she had been. Frank was dead, and it sent a shiver down her spine.

Suzann remembered Tobias describing how the spirit, after death, floated in coloured raindrops for those who knew it, to catch or let disappear, into eternity. Without a word being spoken, she understood that Frank's spirit was with her, invisibly imbibing her with his coloured raindrops.

She smiled. Her child was saved from the abortion clinic when they switched on the TV. She got up and started pacing the floor.

"How many arguments have we had, Marina, about this unborn child? There will be no abortion clinic today or ever. Life has made the decision for me. I may have wanted the opposite, but this child must live. You said it might be a magical child. We shall see if it is."

"It will be," stated Marina with surety. "It's the right and only decision."

Suzann walked to her fridge and opened it. She pulled out a bottle of champagne.

"I know Frank's dead, but he liked his champagne. We should stay here, drink and celebrate what remains inside me."

Marina smiled and took the glass proffered by Suzann:

"His soul may rest, but not leave us," she said.

They clinked their glasses together and drank deeply toasting Frank and the life he left behind, in Suzann.

28

Malcolm was in his study as usual. One thing that remained after his brush with mortality was that working today, in order to secure a better future, was a myth. Better, he concluded, to spend more time on *being* today. Tomorrow is destined to one day be no more. This realisation lifted his spirit. He returned to work at NYU, but only on a part-time basis.

During his recovery he studied all of Tobias' writings, which he had retrieved in Maine. Their content seemed to strike a chord with his heart. The writing was like a key, opening up an inner route to a font of knowledge, from which he felt compelled to drink. He quickly learnt that to satisfy this thirst was no easy task.

As he had with 'The Light' so he did with Tobias' notebooks. He considered them like ancient scripts, whose knowledge was only opened to those able to receive it. He started incorporating them into his fortnightly lectures, which remained popular. Malcolm was completely engrossed by the project. He compiled the hand-written work into some form of digital order. This task dominated his attention to such an extent he became almost reclusive.

And so he practiced for his next lecture:

"The solidity of the world we perceive is entirely dependent on the speed we travel in the slipstream of time, 22,000 miles per sec. All energy travelling at less than that speed materialises in some form or the other, and it has nothing to do with humans. Why do we see life as a competition? Life is not a competition. It is not a football match."

He practiced a dramatic pause before proceeding:

"All the comparative states, good, bad, black, white, right and wrong all assume a perfection no one achieves, how can they? Whoever makes a judgement on another, creates war. There is only one certainty in this life. One day there will be a moment where there isn't another moment. We will all die, and we must face our own death, not try to hide and hitchhike, onto a pickup truck of tomorrow."

Malcolm sat back trying to digest the vividness of impressions the words might conjure up for his students.

They put Jung in the shade.

There was a knock at the door. He was expecting it. Marina entered, and they hugged each other fondly. She had bought flowers. Their scent invaded his manly space.

"Amazing," he said sniffing their perfume. "How is Suzann?"

It had been some months since Frank died.

"She looks good but she's still very upset. It was no more than a whim, my suggestion… you guys came to Maine and look at the consequences. I've learnt things happen I can do nothing about. Part of me feels responsible for the journey we all took."

"Everyone thinks they play an important role, Marina and I mean that in the nicest possible way. We all do it, like it or not. We are all responsible and at the same time we have no responsibility, says Tobias in his writing. That reminds me; these are for you."

He went to his desk and picked up three large books. He handed them to her. Marina looked back at Malcolm quizzically, as he explained:

"Those are Kimi's books. They are not for me, but for you, that is for sure."

"I'm so happy you are doing this," Marina replied gently.

She searched his eyes for any desire. It was not there. She felt similar with Tobias. It didn't matter that she was unable to recall events that took place in those two nights, alone with him.

She was unsure with Malcolm, but sensed a togetherness with him that went beyond normal intercourse. She felt safe.

"Money is no secret, more an open book," remarked Malcolm, seriously. "Without 'The Light' being written and attracting us, we would not be here, now. Suzann's Frank may be still alive. We would never have met. I, certainly, might be dead. It is chaos theory. The butterfly effect, quantum mechanics and I couldn't be doing what I'm doing, without your help," he added, gently.

"It's mutual Malcolm. You're teaching me like I'm one of your students. You don't know it. I'm learning a new craft." She pointed at the books he gave her earlier. "Yet before I make a real practice of my craft, I need to ensure the survival of Suzann and her child. After that, my inner sense tells me it will be a different matter."

Her phone rang. She answered:

"Sure," she said. "I'm on my way now. I'll be home in twenty minutes." The call ended.

Marina stood up and picked up the books.

"I have a feeling these are going to be an inspiration. That was a client. Soon I'll be busy as a healer rather than a financier. It will be more satisfying in the long run. I will see Suzann later. She's been out today. First time this week and wants to tell me all about it."

Marina was on her way to the door as she spoke. She swiftly put on her coat, kissed him lightly on both cheeks and disappeared down the corridor.

With a sigh, Malcolm returned to the task in hand. He opened one of the notebooks at random. He sat down and started reading. Once more he ventured into another dimension.

29

Suzann debated what to tell her husband, Paul, about her pregnancy. How could she do that? Imagining the scene brought shivers down her spine. She tried to dismiss it but found she only replaced one horrific fantasy with another.

An image jumped into her mind of Frank's last moments. It was even darker than her nightmare of a potential confrontation with her husband. It almost overwhelmed her entirely.

The irony, as she discovered from numerous hours' research on the internet, was that Frank and the film 'Saturn and Satan', had achieved cult status. The movie was a blockbuster success, because of Frank's unforeseen doom. Groups denying his death or creating mythical conspiracies, sprung up. This transformed Frank into a momentary legend, lining the pockets of the box office. His nomination for 'best supporting actor' at the Oscars was destined for certain success.

In fact, Suzann was about to distract herself, by searching Google to catch the latest on him, when the phone rang.

"Suzann. Can we meet up?"

"Tobias!" she exclaimed, shocked.

"I'm in town and wanted to talk with you."

"Like to come over?" she asked.

"Can you come to visit me? Just grab a cab. It might do you good to get out?" he suggested.

"Sure. Where are you?"

"222 West 23rd. I'll meet you in the lobby?"

"OK. I'll be there in an hour. Text you, if I have a problem."

"I look forward to it, see you soon," replied Tobias.

Forty minutes later, dressed and ready, Suzann stopped a yellow taxi and got in.

"222 West 23rd please."

"You mean the Chelsea," said the driver with a smile.

It was cold with winter well on the way. Suzann watched the people hurrying along the sidewalk, huddled against the zero temperatures. Snow was predicted but she felt warm, observing the rushing city, as they crossed over Times Square and closed in on 23rd.

Fifteen minutes later Suzann sat on a bench in the empty lobby. There was plenty of activity, as various workmen from the vast ten-storey building, passed her by. They were working on the renovation of the renowned hotel.

The sounds of their construction resonated round the empty walls, which for some reason she imagined as being filled by a variety of strange, surreal paintings. It was eerie. She wondered, after a few minutes, if she was in the right place.

From nowhere, she heard her name being called. She looked in the direction of the voice. It was Tobias, dressed in his customary long white robe and multi-coloured hat, his arms open, in a warm welcome:

"Come, come," he said, taking her hand. He led her up the long, winding, art deco staircase. They ascended four floors, walked along a corridor and Tobias opened a door to one of the rooms. They entered.

Once inside, she felt she was in another world. It was quiet, tastefully decorated and homely. She sat on a cosy sofa and looked through the French windows that led to a small balcony. Tobias made tea.

"One of the things I love about New York is that you never know when you go into a building, where it will take you. Here is a great example. This room belongs to a girl called Juliana. She owns the lease on this for life. She thought that meant *her* life, not the life of the person she signed the lease with. Stanley Bard is dying but shouldn't terminate their agreement. Still, new owners disagree. Juliana is not alone so there are battles to come," observed Tobias, passing her tea.

"You didn't invite me here to talk about that," retorted Suzann.

"No, you're right. The history of the Chelsea though, is an added extra and a good metaphor for who I am. Compared with the big cities of Europe, NYC is new and without so many experiences, yet there are plenty of ghosts at the Chelsea Hotel. I like that.

"People talk of the myths of Warhol, Dylan, Brendan Behan, Tom Wolfe and so many others, who all must have had a debt or two to Stanley Bard or his father. Now he's passed on. I like the dead in the living. That's got something to do with why you're here. You, literally have the dead alive, within you."

The walls were solid, and sound proofed so only vague, dulled noises broke the silence of Tobias's pauses. Suzann noted the complex rose-bush form of the steel works on the terrace border. The winding, dark solid form of such delicate subject matter wove a subtle figurine, mesmerising her.

"I saw Frank the night he died at the opening of the film. We had quite a conversation about you." Tobias spoke as if there was nothing unusual about his admission.

"Oh my God!" exclaimed Suzann. "Why didn't you tell me earlier?"

"There was no need nor is there anything we can do about it now, or then. If Frank had lived, the life inside you would be dead. I'm sure of that. Also, he was not for you. As a long term relationship, you were continents apart. Anyway, why mourn one who will continue through you? Imagine all was darkness before everything began at once. Suddenly one tiny atom of white light appeared in the whole of the cosmos. Before this, there was no darkness, for how could it be dark, without light?

"Bang. All and everything began hurtling galaxies into infinity. If that is the case, then death is not death, merely further evolution. It's possible."

"Do you believe in the living dead?" responded Suzann, trying to follow.

"It might be that we are the living dead. Very few believe it and even less know it."

There was a silence.

Through the glass veranda doors that led to the balcony Suzann saw tiny snowflakes gently fluttering earthward. They reflected her mood of softness and vulnerability. She had an idea that a form with less matter had more power. It calmed her.

"Frank wasn't right for you spiritually. Physically, you were a ripe pair," continued Tobias, laughing.

"But there are several reasons I invited you here. Firstly, your child will be born to represent many. Some things I already know. I need you to follow what I ask. Otherwise, nothing will work out, including my own fate," explained Tobias raising an eyebrow.

"Such as?"

"Try to have the child at the house in Maine. I think that's another few months looking at you. Just a sec, I must give you the key.

"I'll send you the email of two women I know in Purgatory. Mary. You met her. She can help. Someone checks the house every week anyway.

"Marina. You must take her with you. She'll deliver the baby. I'll be there as well, in some form or the other. When you have the child, we all move on up one level. In terms of what space we offer.

"You worry. Let's speculate. You tell Paul you're pregnant with Frank's child. You fight and argue but after a few days you will work out a compromise. You've been married a long time. If I want to think like a normal person, well, DNA puts a financial price on your child, which is on the increase, with each person who pays for 'Saturn and Satan.'

"Until death there is only life, even for ghosts. When life seems crazy, who knows where the madness is manifest? Perhaps, everything is back to front. Too much sanity may be insane? The maddest a human being can do is see life as it is. Not as it's dreamt up to be. Enjoy being pregnant. Speculate!" advised Tobias.

He stood up with a grin and lifted his arms in the air, before lowering himself down again with a cough.

"Are you okay?" She asked.

"Sure. I'm as well as all the ghosts who have lived in this hotel since its 'Speakeasy Days.' After all, those French and Irish poets, painters and pugilists had to have somewhere to get a drink once they hit Manhattan. Listen to their hum through the silence."

He paused and with him, the whole world.

"It is here and now to be with being. It takes work to be with yourself, let alone a ghost. Every being is beyond the past and before the future. Time dictates us, nothing more," concluded Tobias, gently.

His voice seemed to swirl her out of a vortex into which she might have disappeared totally, had he not spoken. With his words, the world ceased to pause. Her perceptions once more woke to the solid world around her. Still the moment resonated deeply within her leaving a permanent mark. A feeling enhanced by Tobias's oblique remark:

"Furnish your depths to fill the tomb; with gifts to bear, into the womb."

There was a gust of wind that drew Suzann's eyes to the small balcony, where a plant swayed and danced in the heightened breeze. Snow was falling now, rhythmically, and for some unknown reason, she felt that she and her unborn child were part of some ritual, which she could not fathom.

She felt calm, warm and comforted, but haunted.

"I was going to go to the hospital to have the child. Do you think Marina will want to be a midwife?" Suddenly doubts flooded in.

Tobias laughed.

"You can doubt but you have no choice. You are part of a cosmic wheel. Everyone gets a turn. In you, it is the most visible and solid, but at the other end of the scale, it is invisible and liquid, yet all are so affected by the same occasion. I'm not predicting, just offering and I almost forgot."

He picked up his phone and studied it.

"There you go," he added. "Just sent you those two email addresses in Purgatory."

The beeping on her phone somehow broke the spell. She picked it up and noticed that three hours had passed in the blink of an eye.

Tobias read her thoughts:

"Time doesn't exist here in the normal way. It has something to do with the space. Seriously, I know you have to go and so do I."

"You're very understanding," she replied.

"Thank you," Tobias replied and then he added, slightly obliquely:

"I won't see you again."

"But you said at the birth," she protested.

"That's another matter and a quantum leap away. You will see me in your child," he stated with certainty.

"Now come," he added, "and don't forget this." He handed her a key. "It's for Maine."

She stood up, took the key, thanked him and together they left the room; to descend the steel rose embellished stairway, avoiding, carefully, the varying construction projects in progress. Somehow the presence of death, in such a live spirit of a building, became absurd to Suzann. The empty walls and lobby became energised with what Tobias termed 'voiceless beings.'

She felt comforted by them.

Tobias escorted her through the light smatterings of snow to 23rd street and saw her into a cab. He watched it disappear into the city fog, before returning to Julia's room in the Chelsea Hotel.

30

Malcolm sat in Washington Square Park, amongst the pink blossoms and fragrant flowers of spring. The archway at the park's entrance was a perfect frame for the not so distant Empire State Building. It reminded Malcolm of Paris and the Arc de Triomphe.

He basked in the success of his morning lecture. His use of Tobias' writings had tempted several psychology schools to offer research grants. Certainly, the content of his lectures got the students' attention. They were unpredictable and fun with a strange originality.

Always after a lecture at the university he would come to Washington Square Park. He would sit for at least fifteen minutes, before slowly ambling through the village to his apartment. In the winter it was cold and bleak but now, he watched spring bursting forth. He contemplated life's fragrance, feeling pleased with himself.

He took a deep breath and began to write in his notebook:

'Winter invisibly morphs into spring. No one can put a finger on how it takes place. The change of seasons is, paradoxically, both too slow and too quick for recognition by the human eye.'

"Hello," interrupted someone.

He looked up and saw a group of six students.

"That lecture you gave this morning," enthused one of the young men, "it amazed me."

"I never thought that thought might think a thought, without a human brain being involved. I mean, to me, that's psychedelic thinking." The woman who spoke laughed at the pun.

"Do you really believe there is a metaphysical equivalence to the Theory of Relativity?" asked another.

Malcolm didn't want to get involved. The lecture was over. Although his rising reputation for radical thought flattered his ego, he wasn't going to get carried away. He got up and smiled:

"Just keep an open mind, which is very difficult in a world where don't know, didn't know and was put in a pot of oil and boiled!" He said, obscurely and stood up.

They looked at him quizzically. He picked up his shoulder bag, and said:

"See you at the next lecture." He turned south, towards his loft near the Bowery.

It was on the corner of Mott and Prince Street, outside the Little Cupcake Bakery, that Malcolm saw Tobias. He was lolling on one of the outside benches. He wore his long white djellaba, dark glasses and a Kashmiri cap

"Hey. I've been waiting all my life in this sun for you," he laughed, getting up.

Malcolm smiled: "Come on, not long now!"

They walked down Mott Street, near Broome and into one of the many converted warehouses, which housed Malcolm's little loft. The sun poured through the arched windows, which stretched from floor to ceiling. It threw beams of geometric light abstractly over the wooden floors and walls, illuminating the dancing city dust.

Malcolm made coffee as Tobias settled into an old chair. Once he had served his companion Malcolm sat opposite. For thirty seconds they shared a silence, which is no easy task.

"Once Suzann has had her baby this may all change," said Tobias. He opened his hands and his eyes wandered, dispassionately over the space.

"I'm not sure about that. My lectures have become a feature at the university."

"Don't turn into a peacock. You can't afford to and I don't mean financially. It's too 'earthy', too solid for a man of liquidity. Be a man who goes with the flow and remember your hero Jung. Alchemists seek for hints and in the dark of light they draw the dragon's breath."

The movement of Tobias's fingers and hands in the sunbeams seemed to enhance the point he was making.

"All that dark unconscious speculation is over for me," stated Malcolm, only half hearing.

"Is it? I wonder? What will happen when you become like me?"

"What do you mean?" interjected Malcolm.

"When Suzann has her baby, then everyone destined to be involved will get a shift and that includes you. We can imagine, why not? For instance, I may be visible to you but not to everyone. Of course, we have been together. You have seen me with Marina and Suzann therefore I exist; anyone and everyone assumes so.

"But we know, as you lectured today, the world of quantum mechanics reveals parallel dimensions to our own. It acts at the same time. Maybe some people exist, or appear, in two dimensions at once. Even in today's digitally-marked world there are maybe those wandering around with no identity. It explains man's fascination with vampires."

"I'm not sure," said Malcolm, "whether you believe what you say, or just make it up!"

"You are never sure. You are inquisitive but when your question is presented with an unusual answer you dispute it."

There was a long, silent pause.

"All is fine," continued Tobias. "For a man with a social security number. Yet imagine—and it is only imagining, that I occupied another dimension and, to get to another dimension, you had to replace me in the dimension I occupy now…That might change many things for you."

Again, Tobias surveyed Malcolm's home, his eyes searching the room.

"It was an excellent lecture you gave today. Nothing like challenging old assumptions."

"Your notes inspire me. They help. I've been able to develop and establish radical alternatives to standard theories. My agent tells me it's worth big bucks." said Malcolm.

"Never assume, I was taught as a child. Always be prepared for what is beyond the imagination. In many ancient societies, especially in the East when a man grew wise he withdrew from society. He makes it hard for others to make him reveal his knowledge. Do not forget Marina and Suzann.

Your meeting them in the café changed all your lives. Your interaction with them is vital whatever your form. But I've come to say goodbye," said Tobias.

"Goodbye?" repeated Malcolm curiously.

"I'm going to Bali tomorrow."

"But," he protested, "what about the project?"

"You will be fine without me. You will have a special role with Suzann's child and I want you to give this to Marina. He handed Malcolm a long, heavy, oblong object.

"What is it?" asked Malcolm. "I would not be in the position I'm in without Marina and Suzann," Malcolm stated. "They are rarely out of my mind."

"It's a carpet. I said earlier all will change with the birth. Every being gets a turn. You will step into another space, another dimension. These lectures you give are an instruction to yourself; for that you read my notebooks, not to profit mankind.

"But I must go and there are never real goodbyes."

Tobias stood up and so did Malcolm. They hugged each other.

"Remember always," said Tobias at the door, "there is real magic in the world. Always trust in it, however weird it appears and don't forget that carpet!"

He winked at Malcolm. In a flash he was gone.

31

It was the summer of 2015. The New Hampshire heat mellowed with the onset of evening. The restorative, re-energised power Marina felt gave her a sense of security and purpose. She surveyed the twenty-five other faces at the table. Marina tingled inside, exhilarated, for she could see her first healing workshop had been a great success.

In the past nine months, her natural talent for perceiving life in simultaneous dimensions had flourished. It was no longer restricted by the officialdom and superficiality of financial markets. Her path and direction were still a gamble but the gamble was more genuine. She was no longer reliant on her knowledge of the fluctuation of currencies.

Marina had learnt to trust instinct and her obliqueness of perception. It opened an insight to another's anxiety and stress. Often her observations awoke in a client an ability to see their own situation in another light and, consequently, a weight was lifted from their shoulders.

It had been an intense week, with no outside communication and based on the principles of 'knowing yourself' through self-observation. The emphasis was on a physical, mental and emotional intensity, stimulated by a combination of events, designed for this purpose.

It was the final evening meal of the workshop. Tomorrow morning everyone would depart. The mansion would become empty again, until the owners found further use for its beautiful space.

Marina experienced waves of emotion course through her being. She felt soft, tender and open. It was this vulnerability, she was beginning to realise, which the cold, harsh, hard world of business had buried. It was only now being reincarnated as she developed herself.

At the other end of the table, in the stillness of the group, Tony Grogan lifted his glass to her.

In Manhattan Tony had an incompatible word of mouth reputation, for his healing through Music Resonance. He met Marina at a downtown workshop. They instantly found their work was complementary and harmonious. He cajoled and motivated her to combine with him on this week. He was proud of his achievement.

He stood up and spoke:

"I just want to thank each and every one of you, for your contribution. I know from experience these weeks can bring an intensity and openness to those brave enough to participate. Tomorrow we go back to our normal lives, which will slowly seep back into our being. This week and all you have learnt you must store within you. Make it a secret light in any potential darkness.

"But before then I want to thank Marina. I sense we all do, for her work and giving. She has illuminated us all in a way that will certainly resonate for a long time."

Tony lifted his glass and all eyes turned to Marina. You could sense the gratitude.

He continued:

"Try to hear your own voice. Not make others hear yours as you listen to no one. Don't be worried by politicians and their Whigs, sing silently your own tune."

He stopped speaking. The silence deepened.

Suzann who sat next to Marina, felt her baby moving. Her time was close. The child was taking the essence of the words into her womb. She felt a satisfaction as if she bore a being that represented so much more than her. The call of night creatures, the slight swish of the breeze, under the canopy of a star-filled universe, gave her a sense of extraordinary peace.

"Remember the here and now we find ourselves in," toasted Marina. She drank deeply, an act which stimulated everyone to follow suit.

Tony's partner, Danny, drained his glass of wine. He clapped his hands.

"Now, all those helping serve the food, you must come with me." He turned to Tony and continued in a loud voice.

"What you said, Tony, was so romantic. If you weren't gay, I'd say love was around the corner!" Danny laughed.

The intensity of the situation dispersed. His remark broke the spell and the celebration of their final meal together, began in earnest.

It was some hours later that Marina and Suzann parted company and went to their separate rooms.

"It's been a great week. A big week for you," said Suzann. "I think instead of going back to Manhattan tomorrow, you and I should go to Maine. It's a feeling I have," added Suzann.

She touched her swollen tummy. "Tobias gave me the keys maybe for a moment such as this? The baby wants to go. Feel." She placed Marina's hand on her stomach.

"Wow, Suzann, you are so full of surprises and very persuasive. I don't know what to say. Let me sleep on it. Did it just move?" Marina asked.

"Yes," replied Suzann and kissed her goodnight.

The relief of success in her new venture had left Marina tired. It opened a host of new vistas. There were possibilities that she needed to contemplate and meditate on. Her new career was about to go onto another level.

Perhaps, she thought, as she slipped between the sheets, Suzann was right and a visit to Maine might be a good idea? She felt an urge to revisit.

In no time at all she was asleep. Instantly she awakened in another dimension.

She was in a room that reminded her of Malcolm's apartment. She sat in a comfortable Victorian chair upholstered with flowered tapestry. Opposite was Tobias who spoke gently:

"The only way to make sense of change, Marina, is to dive in. Move with what is happening and join the dance. You are a very good dancer. You are beauty personified but still have little patience, for solitaire.

"See yourself a year ago as a caterpillar. Now you are a chrysalis, soon to be a butterfly. You are the catalyst of this cosmic shift, bound hand and foot by fate. They open in you, what some call chakras and others call karmas.

"You are filling Kimi's space, making use of the wisdom she acquired." Tobias concluded. He grinned and leaned forward. He was holding a long cardboard tube that obviously contained something. She wondered what it was.

"There is a map in here," he said, handing it to her.

The room in which they sat started to dissipate and become atomic. Yet she could distinguish a molecular form of a billion tiny points that represented Tobias, rather than him being a solid form. It was the same for everything, even for herself, which made her panic. She seemed to be leaving one dimension and flying back to a more familiar one. The vision became replaced by a gentle compassion she had noted the day before, in the eyes of one of her clients.

The world with Tobias was fading fast, although, as often happens in a dream state, he would suddenly reappear, breaking some sleep-filled imagery with his hand, waving the rolled up map, as an indication to never forget.

Slowly, with no warning, morning broke into this other dimension, disturbing Marina's slumber. Despite the intensity of her dreams, she woke feeling refreshed and ready for the day ahead.

They had agreed, as part of the workshop, to leave silently without goodbyes and so Marina quickly prepared herself, packed her bags, left the room and went in search of Suzann.

She found her ready, smiling and blooming, in the hallway. Marina took her bag and they walked into the sunshine.

Danny and Tony were there, and they kissed them goodbye, leaving the men, as arranged, to deal with locking up.

They got into Marina's car. She looked over at Suzann:

"So next stop Purgatory, Maine, is that right?" she asked with a smile.

"I knew you'd say that. It won't take more than a couple of hours," added Suzann.

"Let's go. Can't wait to get there," said Marina. She started the engine and they drove off, towards the highway.

32

One week after Marina and Suzann arrived in Maine, Malcolm made plans to join them. A series of digital communications let him know the birth was imminent.

As evening wore on he reflected on his busy day. The physical and mental exertion left him tired and anxious about the journey, so he decided an early night was in order.

Malcolm wasn't feeling very well. He decided to take two of his prescribed painkillers. It was a form of medication he usually avoided, but the stress of the day coupled with an ache in his left side, made it unavoidable. After ingesting the substance, it always led to a series of surreal states of varying intensities, which could profoundly affect his level of consciousness.

He sat down in his favourite chair, as the evening began flickering shadows, on the tall walls of his loft. He lit a candle on the table next to him. It sent a warm, soft light, round the room. Malcolm studied the flickering flame and got drawn into a world which took his mind rolling back the years, till a lavish memory appeared.

He was transported back to his mother's death. He remembered preferring to go into her neglected garden, rather than stay with his bereaving family.

'She,' he thought, 'would prefer me to dead-head the rosebushes.'

As he chopped a withering rosehip, his mother came to him very clearly and said:

"That's what I've done Malcolm. I've dead headed myself, so you and your sister can get more energy from the root."

He sat up with a start at the recollection, jerking his head backward, for he was wondering more on what his memory conjured up, than where he was and what he was doing now, in New York. It took longer than he expected to come back to reality, which was worrying.

He could hear the tick-tock of his heart.

Outside, the luminescence of the night slowly dawned. The sun slid away westward and in its place, came the darkening realm of night, with its dominating, watery moon, for guidance.

Malcolm thought of making coffee. He felt so tired and lethargic. However, he was comfortable in his chair and the medication had worked. It washed away his aches and pains. He felt his tensions melt and he began to relax.

His lids drooped again, and his eyes started closing, only to wake in the world of dreams, where the vague corridors of time and space melted and merged into a surreal reality he only half understood. He approached this different world, as he began to slumber.

Maine came into his view.

He had a sense of Marina. He felt their fates were entwined.

A series of visages, faces on faces, flashed on his inner eye. All the women whom he had ever loved seemed to dance before a flickering fire of his emotion. The flames burning his heart to ashes; yet the vision, suggesting some form of alchemy, turning base metal to gold.

'Was there any hope?'

The question gave him a taste in his mouth that led him to a conversation, which took place twenty-five years previously.

He was in San Francisco, taking coffee with his tutor, a small man, always immaculately dressed, in complete contrast to his radical mind. He was not a well man either. His proximity to death gave him an edge on the present, usually avoided by other people.

He leaned forward, one hand on his ornate walking stick, his blue eyes intensely mesmerising the young Malcolm:

"I mean," he said, opening his other hand. "If a butterfly were to land on my palm and I make a fist, the butterfly dies. Remember that in life Malcolm, especially with women."

The perception of the moment scared Malcolm. He had difficulty extricating himself from the recollection. He struggled to come back to New York.

The symmetry of sunset angled and diffused by the Manhattan skyline, gave him a sense of safety, of knowing where he was, although the way he had travelled in time disturbed him.

"Where are you now?"

Malcolm instantly recognised Tobias's voice.

He was sitting opposite. How he got there didn't concern Malcom in the slightest. In fact, unexplained presence of Tobias brought him back. It gave him a security that had not been there, since self-medicating:

"Reality," continued Tobias with a slight grin, "for you is becoming replaced by, how shall I put it?" He paused, looking to pluck the words from the invisible, "an unconscious intercourse with nature. It is as old as creation itself. Now is almost time to stop drinking in that pure organic pleasure. You will be hidden by wreathes of mist that mystify minds. A caterpillar and chrysalis live much longer than the butterfly."

"What is happening?" Malcolm asked.

"Everything is happening," responded Tobias with a wink.

"I'm not feeling so well," Malcolm admitted. "But if you stay, we could go together to Purgatory tomorrow."

"I know," replied Tobias, "I'll tell them."

"What?"

"You couldn't make it," again he smiled.

"What is so amusing?"

"Everyone gets a turn. We like to think we do but doing does what doing does. Things are done. Being born, growing up, falling in love, making children, growing old, dying; these things we do not do, they are done.

"Think carefully. Our spiritual presence is helping a child into the world. If it is destined, then you and I get a turn too. A rebirth of sorts and how is it manifested? How does it take place? Well I do not know any more than you."

"Marina has given me real strength," Malcolm interrupted.

Suddenly, he had an acrid, strange taste in his mouth.

The room became three months ago. He was with Marina. They were laughing and close. He felt the warmth of their completeness envelope him. There was a harmony and togetherness, between them. As if for a moment, they were two streams merging into a river, before their tributaries parted and they separated, went on their own flow.

It had been a rare and beautiful moment. Marina broke it, getting up and offering to make tea, in order to break her own spell.

"These will all pass to you when I move on," he had said to her, indicating the notes, he was working on.

"You're not moving anywhere," Marina replied, pouring water into the cups.

"Where are you now?" The repeated question called him back to the present once more.

"You cannot dream about Marina or Suzann or anyone, anymore," Tobias advised.

"You will no longer dream in the way you have done in the past. After tonight, you will be making some changes. You've had everything necessary for this extravagant journey of life and you've spent it. You think you chose, when the choosing was done for you. Yet you have time left like I did some two years ago, when I was in your position."

"How do you mean?" asked Malcolm, despite the blurring of his vision.

Suddenly he was awake and back in his room. Night had crept in without warning. The hues of evening had turned light blue, with the rising of the moon, in a dark ocean lit by vague stars, glistening behind the city illuminations. Malcolm stood and looked out, over to the horizon that never ceased to amaze him. It was late enough for bed and his ghostly apparitions, real or unreal, no longer concerned him.

In the distance he heard a saxophone play.

He thought of the next day. He felt comforted, in his mental haze, that Tobias, might be with him.

"One moment here, next moment gone will the space ship pick you up, as you said it would?" asked the apparition of Tobias.

Malcolm wondered whether the painkillers were causing hallucinations.

"Weird," he said, getting up. He went to the bedroom, closing the door and lay down.

Almost instantly he fell asleep.

He stood before a great ocean. He had a sensation of starting something new that he had never tried. These were uncharted waters and the result of all he had learnt in life.

Nothing intentionally educated in him led him to where he was. It was the stranger interactions in life that mapped his journey, towards this endless sea.

He had tried so hard to be an individual of importance and now he was no longer of any importance. It meant nothing; even ownership had no place on this star, to which this ocean would take him.

He would just move forever, as is the law for all souls, whatever their religion.

We are all, only a point of one.

A sensation of passing, poured over the shoreline and each atom, was like a rebirth.

He knew everything and nothing, for he sensed, the outer life we humans think we control and hold so sacred, was written before anyone spoke a word.

Only the exploration of one's unique, inner universe has any real value over a lifetime.

There was only this. He realised death was made myth by a rebirth, etched forever on this endless ocean of emotion, before which Malcolm stood.

Then he knew no more.

33

Marina, dressed in a light frock, cardigan and large, floppy hat, looked out across the still, uninhabited lake. She liked to be with people, yet so often found herself to be alone. Somehow, she felt a parallel in her life with the vast empty forests and landscapes of New England, for beauty contributed to both their desolations. Her solitary idyll of an afternoon was held in a silence, only disturbed by the shrill, call of:

'Loon. Loon. Loon,' resonating over the waters.

She remembered the call of a rare, odd and mysterious bird, known as a loon. They arrived annually in the spring and during the summer months, came to nest and breed on the lake. Their notes echoed over the waters. Once the days grew shorter, they were gone with their distaste of dark nights turning the waters into a mass of crackling ice crystals. Now though, their migration was in the future.

It had been a good idea of Suzann's, Marina reflected, to come here before returning to the city. It gave her space to digest the intricacies and content of her workshop.

Marina remembered how innocently she came here to visit Tobias and had stepped through a portal, from which there was no return.

She sensed the ghosts of the ancient Algonquin tribe, who lived in these forests for thousands of years, before civilisation arrived.

A sharp breeze sprang up and she pulled her cardigan closer. Evening was near, and a huge white moon hung in the sky. The chill reminding her that midsummer was over.

Her phone beeped, and she picked it up to read the message.

"Sorry for the delay but we are on our way. Love Tobias."

It was vague in terms of timing, but she got up and went inside to tell Suzann.

"No problem. It'll be a reunion of sorts when he and Malcolm get here. I feel really comfortable," she said as she lay on the sofa.

Suzann was wholly concentrated on her child inside. It felt there was so much more than her physical presence involved. Somehow, the culmination of her life was in the moments ahead. She felt the baby kick in her tummy and grimaced.

"All okay?" asked Marina.

"It's just a twinge," responded Suzann.

"Let me know if you feel anything out of the ordinary. Anyway, it should be at least another week. I can't see any need to worry."

"Tea?" interrupted a voice.

It was Dorothea, who looked after the house when it was unoccupied. She had volunteered, considering Suzann's state, to look after them, while they stayed.

She came in carrying a tray and talking:

"You know Marina, Purgatory, Maine was so named because an invading British Colonel came here. He thought he'd found heaven until the mosquitoes appeared, which he thought made it hell. So, he called it Purgatory. A place for lost souls caught between two worlds. Mind you, you're lucky. It's too late, by a month, to be plagued by the mosquitoes."

"And we must be gone soon as well I guess. Otherwise, Suzann's going to be so big she won't be able to get in the car," joked Marina.

"They say a child born by the lake is like a loon born here. It will always find a way home. Better to come into the world with nature than in a clinic in the city. That's what I say but then I'm just a country girl. In Maine, we cover all the bases," she concluded, pouring tea.

"Ahh!" cried Suzann.

"What is it?" said Marina.

Suzann sat up and felt her bulging tummy:

"Another twinge. They're becoming regular."

"Hey, let me feel," said Dorothea calmly, walking over and touching her abdomen.

"You've started," she declared with a glint in her eye. "And you are going nowhere until that child's out of you," she added with certainty.

"Come Marina, rub her back gently. I'll call Mary. She's a midwife." Dorothea spoke confidently.

She switched on a lamp, for dusk was rapidly approaching. Outside, the sun was sinking swiftly. The blue of day was invisibly melting into night, enhancing the moon.

Inside, with the arrival of Dorothea's friend, preparations began in earnest for the delivery of Suzann's baby.

Meanwhile, and on the way to join them Tobias, although driving, still managed to emphasise his words with dramatic gestures.

"And so, it's like I live in a strange world, but I operate in what normal people consider reality. I live in two worlds at once. That's living in a parallel universe. It's ordinary and extraordinary, at the same time.

"Nine-fingered Eddie once said to me in Goa, that birth was merely a representation of an atomic fluidity, in the balanced harmony of a misunderstood cosmic equation. Hey man, I've always loved driving and I shall miss it," laughed Tobias.

"Cheer up it's not the end of the world. Mind you it is the end of one. Every ending must have an equivalent beginning. A man isn't a man until he opens his mouth. I've told you enough," he concluded.

They had just turned west towards Purgatory, their destination. It was dark, but the vast, open heavens were awash with the glitter of stars, pulsating behind the silvery gleam of the full moon.

"We occupy space, which is what all life does. Our existence is to do with what used to be known as keeping body and soul together. It means our atomic structure only gives the appearance of solidity. Ha!" He put his foot down on the accelerator.

"Nothing can happen," said his companion in a resigned voice.

"That's right. Some will see you and others won't. We are just ordinary people, disguised as non-entities, yet for thousands of years those who worship ownership have sought our extermination, whatever our manifestation. Witches, alchemists, radicals; anyone seeking, and not obeying the statute of physical man, is always subject to the torture of their generation."

"What about Frank?" replied his passenger.

"Frank just began in his last life and he has a few more lifetimes to go through before he is sitting in a car like we are. In our dimension, time travels faster. So here I am with you on our way somewhere that we have already arrived at. There are only two more miles in terms of distance."

The aromas of incense and roses pervaded the room where Suzann was giving birth. Time had ceased to exist in Purgatory. Forever this ritual of bearing life into the world had occurred in the space where Suzann lay.

She was no longer in her body.

She felt like she floated above what was happening to her. She was detached. As if she was between the dead and the living. What was taking place within her was making the invisible, visible.

She remembered being with Frank. He was beckoning her to join him somewhere. At the same moment, she felt the pain of the Earth, the whole of Mother Nature pulling her, agonisingly towards the ground. Her eyes filled with whirling hues of colour. During a pause she felt Marina clasp her hand. It seemed Marina gave life with her fingers. Suzann, held by Marina's eyes, trusted their look to show her the way.

Marina was transported by the birth pains of her friend and, although without experience, took complete control of the situation. After Suzann went into labour, Marina felt she became Kimi reincarnated.

It seemed totally natural that her dead friend's knowledge should rise to the fore. She directed Dorothea and Mary, despite not having their experience.

Unexpectedly, Marina, after several hours, found the physical part of the birth, although difficult, nothing in comparison to the change in the atmosphere. She dwelt on the threshold of two dimensions. They parted and interacted, simultaneously.

Suddenly she went back in time. She was with Tobias on his carpet. The stolen moment that always evaded her memory was alive. She revelled in the recollection. In the physical world, Suzann's cervix was opening faster. In Marina's mind, she relived what happened, last year.

She remembered Tobias leading her down toward the lakeside. The dancing lights before her eyes transfixing her with their mysticism. The Aurora Borealis illuminating the skies with their circus show of rainbows cavorting across the heavens.

"A sight not good for the eyes of man, Marina; really a sight only for the eyes of God," remarked Tobias.

"When it is time for you to remember this moment remember also this. There is a power in death to wake a person up. Only after a moment is lived, does one see life and death as the same. No one does anything about anything. It all happens, which is far more frightening than believing one has a choice. You will understand. Everyone gets a turn. Malcolm will step into my shoes," he smiled ruefully.

"We are all waves on an ocean," Tobias added and disappeared.

Marina watched as he dissolved into a billion atoms, which were swallowed up in the cosmic light show before her eyes. She was alone, mesmerised by a flurry of solar winds.

"I can see her head, she's nearly there," said Dorothea.

Marina was back in the room. She was staring into Suzann's eyes.

"One last push," she whispered.

Suzann screamed.

Marina moved her hands and held the new life. It slid into the world. She cradled the little girl gently, then laid her on Suzann's tummy. There was an atmosphere of total peace and tranquillity.

"We shall call her Krystel," said Suzann.

"Yes, beautiful name, rest now," whispered Marina, as she soothed her brow.

Half an hour later the door opened. Malcolm appeared. Marina got up and walked over to greet him:

"I'm sorry we're so late," he said flustered. "I mean I'm so late. You see Tobias."

Marina put a finger to his lips:

"Tobias has gone as we both know. Come in. Your timing is perfect."

34

January 2016, a bright winter's day in New York. Manhattan sparkles like a crystal in the cold sunlight.

The café at 1000 Madison Avenue is quite busy with a number of varied customers.

At one of the tables is a group of three people. They radiate a certain presence, which has a strange kind of attraction.

It is these three atoms of humanity, Malcolm, Suzann and Marina, that our story is about.

Malcolm appeared pale, thin and animated as he spoke:

"You know David told me he was born with the talent to sing in tune. It didn't matter where you were; prison or palace. To sing in tune is an un-buyable gift. Try and hear your own voice. It was good advice."

Suzann interrupted him:

"There is a strange vibe today like the city is in mourning."

"A great man passed on who gave a little bit of himself to everyone who could hear," replied Malcolm.

"It'll be time for you to pass on soon," observed Marina, dryly, with a knowing smile.

"You can't stay in this city too long. Now until we see you again, which I am sure we will, Suzann and I bought you this as a gift."

Marina rummaged in her bag. She pulled out a book and put it on the table.

'The Light,' proclaimed the title.

"Look," Suzann said and pointed at a young girl holding a baby, entering the café.

Malcolm didn't look. The sight of the title before his eyes caused a shift to another dimension.

"Are you all right?" asked Marina, soothingly.

Malcolm swirled and whirled back to the present moment. Instead of a phantasmagoria of events taking place in a microsecond, he felt a momentary dizziness. He threw it off.

"It's okay, you just went very pale," said Marina, gently.

"We thought you were going to faint," added Suzann.

The girl, who Suzann had pointed out, joined them and passed the baby to its mother. Suzann held her up in front of Malcolm gleefully.

"Here she is. Our little Krystel," she said proudly.

The baby looked deeply, yet compassionately, into Malcolm's eyes.